Intruders

Intruders

SHORT STORIES

Mohale Mashigo

PICADOR AFRICA

First published in 2018 by Picador Africa
an imprint of Pan Macmillan South Africa
Private Bag x19, Northlands
Johannesburg, 2116
www.panmacmillan.co.za

ISBN 978-17701-063-3-8
e-ISBN 978-17701-061-4-7

*Two of the stories in this collection first appeared elsewhere in their infancy:
'Manoka' was included in a friend's e-zine in 2017; and 'High Heel Killer' was
published in the* Mail & Guardian *in 2016.*

Editing by Elana Bregin
Proofreading by Kelly Norwood-Young
Design and typesetting by Triple M Design, Johannesburg
Cover design by publicide
Cover image by Shubnum Khan
Author photo by Sydelle Willow Smith

Contents

The Colourful

Author's Note

Intruders: *noun* /**in' tru ː dəz**/

This one is for a girl who always saves a Boy Who Lived; for delicate and invisible boys; lost souls with praying mothers (even a heathen like me has a praying mother); those who raise themselves in a world that doesn't care whether they live or die, the progeny of forgotten legends; those who have lost too much and have nothing but themselves; for young love and old heartbreak; the ones who fall asleep with a man and wake up next to a monster; for monster slayers and makers; for those who were spat out onto the streets; for the weird, the wonderful ... and us, who never see ourselves in the stars but die in seas searching for them. You are everything.

Dedicated to Kamo and Tumi

Afrofuturism: Ayashis' Amateki

Speculative Fiction that addresses African-American themes and addresses African-American concerns in the context of twentieth-century technoculture — and, more generally, African-American signification that appropriates images of technology and a prosthetically enhanced future — might, for want of a better term, be called 'Afrofuturism'.

– MARK DERY
(Black to the Future: Interviews with Samuel R. Delany, Greg Tate and Tricia Rose)

This collection would be incomplete for me if I didn't include stories set in 'the future'. Writing it, I could almost feel Afrofuturism hiding in the shadows, waiting for the right moment to shout, 'pick me'. It is all the rage right now and everybody has his and her own idea of what it is — even when it's some misguided marketing weirdo just wanting to connect with the cool kids (gross).

There are stories that take place in the future but cannot strictly be called Afrofuturism because (I am of the opinion) Afrofuturism is not for Africans living in Africa. This is not meant, in any way, to undermine the importance of Afrofuturism. So why even mention this? Well, it's probably because South Africa is a country that suffers from low self-esteem and too often parrots the United Kingdom and United States of America (hi, Cultural Imperialism) — just hang out in Braamfontein and listen to people talking about 'peng sneakers this, that and the other, bruv'. This is not an indictment on a world that is shrinking (thanks, in part, to social media) or on the laaities (I'm in my mid-30s, so I feel I've earned the right to call them that) — I love young people and am often in need of a Youth Concierge (a term coined by my writing partner, Nomali Minenhle Cele, who is *too* young and enjoys making fun of my 'elderly ways'; it means a young person who helps an 'older' person understand technology, new slang and trends).

I believe Africans, living in Africa, need something entirely different from Afrofuturism. I'm not going to coin a phrase but please feel free to do so. Our needs, when it comes to imagining futures, or even reimagining a fantasy present, are different from elsewhere on the globe; we actually live on this continent, as opposed to using it as a costume or a stage to play out our ideas. We need a project that predicts (it is fiction after all) Africa's future 'post-colonialism'; this will be divergent for each country on the continent because colonialism (and apartheid) affected us in unique (but sometimes similar) ways. In South Africa, for instance, there needs to exist a place in our imaginations that is the opposite of our present reality where a small minority owns most of the land and lives better lives than the rest.

> *I don't think I should, at this time in our history, be involved in a lot of talking and dreaming about the beautiful skies and the moon, and so on, and dreaming about ideal situations when we don't have them. In the very first place I wouldn't have taken to writing. I wouldn't stick to it when it is so difficult. Except for the fact that I see in it some kind of exposure: it gives me the opportunity to expose what we feel inside. — Miriam Tlali (interviewed by Cecily Lockett, 4 September 1988)*

This was my particular challenge when writing stories based in the future. I'm not a fan of dystopia (though sometimes it feels like we are living it) nor am I a believer in utopia; but I do believe that there is a place in between the two where South Africans are able to live in a future that is free from white supremacy (please don't argue with me; I'm not interested in your reverse racism fallacy) and poverty. For me, imagining a future where our languages and cultures are working with technology *for us* in order to, as Miriam Tlali says, 'expose what we feel inside', I had to draw from South African folklore and urban legends. How could I not go back to our amazing stories about mutlanyana (rabbit) outsmarting a hungry lion, for inspiration? Or 'jazz up' urban legends: the headless horse named Waar is my Kop (Where is my Head) that terrorises young children, or the beautiful ghost of a young woman named Vera who haunted the roads of Soweto at night, causing young men to drive off the road?

It was much easier for me to lace up takkies that were familiar and, indeed, 'my size', in order to travel a road unknown. Is the future still filled with (generational) inequality? Are there any smart cities or has corruption stolen the opportunities for young people to influence the direction of technology? If resources and education currently benefit only one group, what does that mean for the use of technology in the future? How does who we are right now affect an imagined future? These are questions that I'm interested in. I'm also interested in who we are now, no matter how unremarkable we seem, under the lens of speculative fiction.

Afrofuturism is an escape for those who find themselves in the minority and divorced or violently removed from their African roots, so they imagine a 'black future' where they aren't a minority and are able to marry their culture with technology. That is a very important story and it means a lot to many people. There are so many wonderful writers from the diaspora dealing with those feelings/complexities that it would be insincere of me to parrot what they are doing.

My story, as an African living in Africa, is this: I lived (as in, under the same roof) with white people for the first time when I was a 19-year-old student. My television screen showed stories populated by black people speaking indigenous languages, so I have never suffered from a lack of representation as such. Was I, though, still living in a country where my culture, language and presence were considered a nuisance? Absolutely!

We are so used to wearing shoes that don't fit us – the shoes that are often so tight that we even stop calling them by their familiar, colloquial names – 'di bhathu' or 'takkies' – and give them a new name adopted from elsewhere. So we walk around with fake swagger, trying to hide that we are wearing sneakers that aren't made for our feet.

In the 1980s South Africa had a genre of popular music called Bubblegum music. One of my Bubblegum heroes was Mercy Pakela, who had a hit song called 'Ayashis' Amateki' – a song about a pair of shoes that was beautiful but too tight for her. The chorus is 'Ayashis' Amateki, this is not my size'. 'Ayashis' Amateki', loosely translated, means the shoes (in this case takkies – what we now call trainers or sneakers in South Africa) are burning my feet – because they are too tight. I wonder sometimes if Mercy Pakela wasn't really a philosopher who was trying, with her hit song, to tell us to remain true to ourselves.

It would be disingenuous of me to take Afrofuturism wholesale and pretend that it is 'my size'. What I want for Africans living in Africa is to imagine a future in their storytelling that deals with issues that are unique to us. I would like for us to see what size takkies fit us, and run with that. It's obviously too late for me to bring takkies 'back' (most of my family still call them that) for cool kids but perhaps there is enough time to stop us from adopting other things that aren't necessarily for us. Whatever you do, do not go and call it something obnoxious like

'Motherland Futurism' – asseblief tog!

May this _____ (insert the name you've all agreed on) also focus on Now and not just The Future. Let us use our folktales if need be – use them to imagine us being fantastical in this Africa we occupy right now. I write for a comic book, *Kwezi*, and I cannot tell you how happy it makes children to see a superhero who looks like them and lives in a country like theirs. Let us be fantastical* right now and in the future, wearing takkies that fit us.

* *fantastical (adj.): conceived or appearing as if conceived by an unrestrained imagination; odd and remarkable; bizarre; grotesque.*

The Good

Manoka

Ndumiso looked shocked. His eyes moved down to my waist and his right hand moved away from between my legs. Fear. His and mine. It was his idea for us to sneak out and take a walk on the beach. Koko, my grandmother, had fallen asleep with my daughter in her arms when the screen on my phone lit up: *Ngingaphandle. Walk on the beach? Wanna be alone.* The answer was always going to be yes. I say 'no' a lot but for him 'yes' tumbled out of my mouth before I even understood what he was asking for.

'Ndumiso, we are here on a church trip. Better not try anything,' I said as we sat down on the wet sand. He placed his hand on my left thigh, exposed through my khanga. Water touched our ankles as I tasted the inside of Ndumiso's mouth: cigarettes and breath mints. All those mornings in church, wondering what it would be like to feel his body pressed against mine. Butterflies and nausea. The lead tenor of the choir with an angelic voice. Erect and eager.

'Why are you crying?'
  'Koko ... I killed him.'
  'Is that why you are crying?'
  'No ... Yes ... I don't know.'
  Koko is telling me that I have to go: 'Take the baby and do as I tell you.' She is tying her doek and putting on shoes. I don't move. 'Why am I the only one who is putting on shoes? You know the truth. It's time to go now. Now, Manoka!' Am I losing my mind? I just told Koko the most unbelievable story. Instead of calling the police or dying from shock, she is calmly putting on her shoes. The gargling sound Ndumiso made comes back to me and I vomit. Brackish water leaves my mouth – no blood in mine, not like Ndumiso as he tried to breathe through bloody, water-filled lungs. 'Manoka!' Koko shakes me. 'We are running out of ...' Her lips are moving but all I hear is the sea and gargling. My

mind is leaving me. It is in the ocean with Ndumiso's body. I pushed it into the water. Well ... the tentacles did.

The sun hasn't yet risen on Christmas morning. Soon someone from our church group will knock on our door to make sure we did not oversleep. Jobs like that were assigned to the teenage members of the congregation. The pastor said we would pray on the beach before sunrise. This whole trip was not meant to happen. I am not religious, neither is Koko. She goes to church without conviction but rather for the company of the church ladies − not that she sees them anymore. Her afternoons now belong to Nkaiseng: my daughter. I am not supposed to be in Durban. None of us is. Koko has never liked these church trips: 'I like praising God with people who love Him. I don't need to travel long distance for that.' Every year the church organises a trip to Durban. This is mainly for church members who don't have family members to celebrate the holy day with. The pastor-in-training/choirmaster is put in charge of the outing, which is what makes it so popular with the youth choir.

When I was younger, Christmas was a lonely time. Koko did everything she could to fill the hole − the parent-shaped hole in my young heart. A hole surrounded by questions: Are they alive?

Do they not miss me? Was the thought of being in my life such a bad thing? Nobody knows who my father is, though not for any lack of trying. I just had one of those mothers who was hard-headed, sharp-tongued and not interested in explaining herself. They must have asked her the question of my paternity until they grew tired of being insulted very personally. My mother walked out one day after declaring that I had 'had enough breast milk to be strong'. She pulled her breast out of my mouth and walked out of my life. Never came back. Christmas time was when other children spent time with their mothers and fathers. There was no school, parents were also on leave (most factories were closed) and families went through cycles of love and hate daily. I didn't have that. Eventually, I grew bigger than the hole inside me. The hole was dwarfed by memories. Koko's love drowned whatever longing I had for Christmas normalcy. Maybe my mother was right – I was strong enough. That kind of separation should have broken me but I managed to sidestep it. The rejection and long-ing now walked alongside me: it was no longer what defined me. 'Lipuo had her reasons. Sometimes it takes many years to understand why our parents do what they do.' That's what Koko always said when I asked her why my mother, Lipuo, left me.

'It's time I tell you why your mother left.'

'Koko, did you hear me?' I couldn't hear my voice but I could tell that I was shouting. Once I emerged from the water, I wasn't sure if I had dreamed what had just happened. I could no longer see Ndumiso's body but the blood on my top removed any doubts I had – he was dead and I had killed him. Somehow I made it back to the holiday apartments, really just old, ugly flats turned into accommodation for holidaymakers. With tears in my eyes, salt in my mouth and fear chasing me, I banged on the door and Koko let me in. Any speech she had practised about unwanted pregnancy and being reckless flew out of the door. The rehearsed words were probably eager to join Ndumiso in the ocean. My grandmother looked at my wet clothes. She wasn't surprised. I collapsed on the floor. A hand stopped my scream from filling the room. 'You have questions … I wanted to tell you tomorrow. There was no privacy on the bus otherwise I would have done it there. Don't be …' Koko's voice croaked and trailed off. She was looking at the blood on my top. Her eyes asked the question we both knew the answer to: Did someone get hurt? I nodded. Koko's hand fell away from my mouth. Another unspoken question. I answered: 'Ndumiso.' Hand on mouth again. 'Sssshhhh. Tell me what happened.'

I got fired. That's what happened. Imran told me that they couldn't afford me anymore. What he really meant was his father's young new wife needed a job. I was a temp anyway. Temps don't need long-term consideration; that's just how it is. Being a receptionist was obviously not meant to be in my future. Imran had always had a soft spot for me, which is why I was allowed to keep my job until bonus time. Koko was amused. 'Temps getting bonuses? It must be your big, beautiful eyes.' My grandmother always complimented my eyes. They were the reason why I was so smart in school, cooked the best morogo she had ever tasted and found her house keys when she couldn't. My eyes also got me into trouble. 'You don't even know who the father of your child is because your big eyes can't focus. You look at all these boys and think you can have them all. Girls with small eyes can't see as many boys as you can, Manoka! You make me tired.' That was the one and only time my grandmother said something negative about my pregnancy. It's been like that as far back as I can remember. I do something that should break my Koko's heart, she is upset, and then it's over. Koko and I somehow had the ability to walk alongside our hurt and disappointment; we never let it get ahead of us or lead us astray. 'Imran says they can't afford me anymore.' Tears were dancing on the edges of my eyes. 'Never mind. I have my pension and I wash and iron clothes. We'll be fine. Imran can keep that job,' she said with a smile.

The trip to Durban was raised one afternoon while I was looking for jobs on my phone while feeding Nkaiseng. Koko came in from visiting a sick church member. 'How is MaSipho?' I asked. Koko untied her doek, another church habit that she did with very little conviction. 'She is old. Old people get sick. So she is fine.' We giggled as Koko looked outside to see if any of our neighbours had heard her. My full name and surname came out of her mouth: 'Manoka Patricia Mashile!' It meant something important was coming. Nkaiseng pressed my nipple between her gums. She seemed to do that when I was anxious. Or maybe I was imagining it. Was my daughter drinking my emotions? Maybe it was like the time I thought her eyes changed colour when I was getting her ready for her bath. Bath time was something that belonged to Koko, not me. After the C-section, getting up and picking my baby up was impossible. Koko took over bath time and never stopped doing it. I was in charge of feeding and changing. I never mentioned the changing eye colour to Koko. It was probably just fatigue that made me think it.

'Is she biting again?'

I nodded, pulling the sleeping baby off my breast.

Koko took a long time to get to her point; that we were spending Christmas in Durban with the church.

'But you always want to spend Christmas here.'

'It'll be a nice change. You worked while you were pregnant and now you can rest.'

'I can rest next year when I look for a job.'

'You've never been to Durban. What kind of young person says no to a trip to the sea?'

'We can't afford it.'

'I'm paying. Are you going to count my money for me? Just say thank you.'

'I don't even attend your church.'

'White people call people who don't have an invitation, like you, a "plus one". You are accompanying me.' Koko laughed and took the baby from my arms. 'Those curtains on the line aren't going to bring themselves in. Hurry up, ngwanyana. It looks like it's going to rain.'

It was raining 'mhhhm's and 'amen, Moruti!'s in church. Koko thought it would be a good idea for me to attend a few times and get to know 'the youth'. A command dressed as half suggestion and half good idea. Church was very similar to a club: stuffy, smelling like burning herbs, with lots of singing and dancing. People were mostly overdressed and pretending to have a good time. Just like with the clubs, I fell in line and obeyed the rules. The Youth Group was very popular, the pride of the congregation; old people loved young people who performed their devotion convincingly. Most of the group was in the choir and ended every utterance with 'God is good'. Christmas suddenly seemed too far away. How could so many people be so insufferable? Nkaiseng was my shield against the 'please join the choir, Sister' requests. I would hold her close and diagnose her with something benign: an ailment that would disappear with a mother's attention, patience and time. Brother Miso – that's what the super-eager members of the Youth Group called him – was the one who finally got me to stay for choir practice. 'Ak'na nkinga Manoka, you can bring Nkaiseng with you.' He smiled and I suddenly had the urge to run my tongue over the gap between his front teeth. 'No, she will cry and ...' Koko hijacked my baby before my lie could take off properly. 'I'll take her.' Away they went, leaving me with Brother Miso and The Insufferables.

That's how I began playing keyboard for the choir. It was one of my silly hobbies, probably the one that got me pregnant. Koko bought it for me when I was 14. She knew that I loved music but couldn't sing. 'Now you will stop breaking glasses with that awful voice of yours,' is what she said when I started crying tears of gratitude. It wasn't my birthday; a gift just because my heart beats. Nobody would ever love me as much as Koko did. 'We will find someone to teach you.' That someone turned out to be Tendai, not much older than me. Tendai's parents were a popular music duo in the 1970s and 80s. Music was not just all around him (multiple plaques of albums sold) but also how he made money. He started giving piano lessons before he got to high school – something his mother loved boasting about. 'Tendi uwonderful watseba? The child surprises me all the time.' Aus' Ntswaki never stopped being a glamorous musician, even though she hadn't performed in years. Particularly fond of shoulder pads and pink lipstick, she often had parties to celebrate her son's every accomplishment. 'So we must be a part of Ntswaki's madness as well?' Koko would ask, every time there was a gathering to celebrate Tendai's next natural childhood milestone. 'Next she will say her child breathes better than others. That poor child.'

He breathed like a normal person. I was trying not to break or scratch anything. 'Relax. Put your hands on the keys. Middle C is this one.' Tendai lifted my hand and let it gently fall on Middle C. I had never been in Aus' Ntswaki's music room. There were trophies and pictures from when she was a singer. Above the piano was a huge photo of her on stage; she had a mic in her hand, long, thin braids and the green sequin jacket she was wearing made me want to burn the torn T-shirt I was wearing. 'Why is your name Tendai?' I moved my hand away from the piano keys. He tilted his head and took my hand back to Middle bloody C again. 'Because my mother gave it to me.' Air left my body slowly. 'Okay, you can ask me anything you like. But I will only answer one question after you play this scale.' CDEFGAB 'My mother played a show in Zimbabwe. Her bass player disappeared, with a woman probably. A young boy named Tendai came to their rescue. He knew all their songs so he played with them for the three nights they were there. My mother says Tendai saved her career. An exaggeration, I'm sure.' CDEFGAB 'Sometimes I just want to be normal. I feel like the other kids pretend to like me but they don't.' CDEFGAB 'You're funny but ... no, I'm not a genius. Your playing has improved already.' CDEFGAB 'Is it true that your mother ran away?' CDEFGAB 'Do you ever feel like you don't belong anywhere?' CDEFGAB 'You have weird eyes. No, not in a bad way. I like them. They sometimes look like water. Don't laugh at me.' CDEFGAB 'My father travels a lot. He is a session musician. Do you ever wonder what your father is like? I wonder what mine is like and I've known him since I was born.' CDEFGAB 'Let's take a break. Come with me to the kitchen to have water.'

I had expected the water to be cold but it wasn't. Like the rest of Durban, it was foreign to me, warm and what I wanted for myself. 'Konje, this is your first trip to Durban. How do you like it?' Ndumiso pulled me closer. 'I haven't seen much of it but I love it.' 'I feel the same way about you.' We both laughed. The water kept inching closer to embrace our legs. The higher up it came, the closer I felt to tears. Was it the moon, humidity or Ndumiso's hand going up my inner thigh? Falling pregnant had made me never want to have sex again. It wasn't from the shame of not knowing who, of the three men I occasionally had sex with, was the father of my child. The choice was not mine; my body simply rejected any kind of sexual activity. Even when I was alone, eyes closed and trying to take the edge off with my right hand, nothing would happen. Arousal wasn't the problem. It was just climaxing and the thought of getting there that had died. Eventually, I became numb when it came to sex. My body

only existed as a vessel for my baby. Lying on the beach with half
of Ndumiso's body over mine, his hand gently stroking me wet, I
was almost on the verge of tears. Eyes closed, I savoured the taste
of Ndumiso's mouth, his neck then his thumb in my mouth. He
pulled himself up on top of me and moaned. At least that's what
it sounded like. I opened my eyes. His face was caught between
confusion and fear. 'Your eyes ...' The way the words came out
of his mouth scared me. Why? I don't know.

'I don't know why she keeps sea water in a bottle.'

Tendai was washing dishes when I asked him about the bottle
of water. The old Coke bottle belonged to his mother and sat on
the window sill in the kitchen. 'My dad had a gig in Cape Town
and she asked him to bring her some.' I had never been to the
sea or anywhere further than the CBD. What did the sea smell
like? Why were people bottling it and keeping parts of it in their
kitchens? Did it have special powers? Why didn't we have any?

'May I smell it?'

Tendai shrugged. His mother wasn't home; he was always
much more relaxed away from her. The cap was stubborn. When
it finally gave, a little bit of the sea splashed on my hands. The
contact made me dizzy. Tendai saw that and took the bottle from

me. Anxiety rose up into my throat. 'Please, pour some onto my hands,' I said, half shouting. I wanted more of that dizzying feeling. We walked over to the sink and he allowed me to hold the ocean above soapy water. Very quickly it slipped through my hands. 'Ma would kill me if she knew I did that.' Tendai kissed me on the cheek tenderly. He did the same thing when we had sex for the first time a few months later. And every time after that. Tendai was my first.

A first-time mom who was too afraid to hold her baby. Nkaiseng was so small but the pain of extracting her kept me from standing up straight. One minute she was inside me and the next she was in the world. A breathing, living person. Koko would take her from me and give her a bath. That was my resting time. Every day I would have the same dream while my grandmother gave my daughter a bath.

In the dream, Koko was in her bedroom, the door closed. Bath-time sounds were lulling me to sleep. Then I'd hear a laugh. Not Koko. A baby's laugh. I instinctively knew it was my daughter. Why didn't she laugh like that with me? There was lots of splashing. Koko is cooing and calling her a good girl. Curiosity leads me to Koko's bedroom door. I want to see my baby smile.

When I open the door, Koko quickly takes Nkaiseng out of the water. 'She'll outgrow it soon.' Koko is holding the baby behind her back. 'Outgrow what?' I'm scared, on the verge of being hysterical. 'Give her to me.' When I finally hold my baby, something terrifies me.

I would wake up before I knew why looking at my baby scared me so much. When I told Koko about the dream, 'It'll go away soon. It's just fatigue,' she said. She was right. The dream eventually went away. But the feeling that something might be wrong with Nkaiseng didn't.

I didn't want anything to go wrong but Ndumiso tried to push me away. He was going to run from me and everything would be different. I tried to speak but my voice got caught in my throat. I wanted to tell him that I hadn't changed. We could work through whatever had scared him. I had never heard bones breaking before but I immediately knew what was happening. Panic set in and I killed him. I promised that I would never kill him again. 'You're killing me, Manoka.' I loved the way he said my name; the boy from KZN twisted it in his mouth and made Manoka sound like music. I preferred it that way: it was a labour of love – music created for me by his mouth and mother tongue. We were sitting on the step outside the house. Koko was visiting sick people with the church ladies. Nkaiseng was crawling not too far away from my feet. A cautious baby, she never strayed far. Ndumiso had just told me that he had feelings for me. 'And how will the women in the choir take this? You're the communal boyfriend, Brother Miso.' We both weren't sure if I was joking or not. 'I'm done with men anyway.' That's when he cried murder. 'You're too young to give up. That's not what God wants for you.' His face was serious.

'Could you ask God to send me an email with a detailed plan for my life ...?'

'Uqalile.' He didn't like it when I was being cynical or blasphemous. I knew how important his faith was, so I stopped. 'Okay. I'll stop killing you.' I meant it. I didn't want to kill him. So why did I?

Why are we doing this? Koko has brought me back to the beach.

'You have to trust me. Haven't I looked after you all your life?' I'm still crying. 'Listen to me very carefully ...' The water we're walking towards is too loud. I can't hear anything my grandmother is saying.

'We have to tell the police.'

Koko has run out of patience. 'These people will kill you.' The sea quietens when she says this. I want to tell her that she is wrong but I'm not sure of anything. My feet tread water and I hold Nkaiseng tighter. Her little eyes are focused on me. Nothing makes sense anymore. Ndumiso's blood has washed away. Like he was never there, not a trace of my sin left. Koko puts her hand on my shoulder. 'I can't go any further.' Her eyes avoid mine.

'But you said all of us ...'

'It's too late for me now. But my time will come again.'

'I've left it too late.' Koko looked annoyed and sad. 'There was never a right time, Manoka.' I had just killed a man; Koko wasn't surprised. Did she always know that I would inexplicably snap and kill someone? Was it because I didn't make friends easily? 'Your mother left because she wanted to be herself.' My mother? Wiping my nose with the back of my hand, I looked up at my grandmother. She was crying. 'There are certain times in your life when your true nature reveals itself. If I had prepared you, none of this would have happened.'

'Will I ever see you again?'

'In the end, I will find my way back.'

'Here?'

'We always find each other.'

Koko is looking down at her feet. She looks happy for a moment. She's up to her ankles in water. The skin on her feet is hardening. Silver scales are forming below her ankles. 'The body remembers,' she whispers sadly. The moonlight reveals webs that have formed between her toes. Three stumps appear on the sides of each of my legs. There is no adrenalin to numb this feeling. It hurts, like glass slicing skin. 'Go, it's getting late,' Koko tells me. I hug my grandmother and walk into the sea. The stumps are growing and I'm unable to stand. The pain is excruciating. Instinctively I shout for Koko. Fear always makes me want to call out for her. 'Trust yourself,' she says. She is crying; I'm not looking at her but I can tell. I crawl into the water and push at it with one hand. Nkaiseng hiccoughs. Her brown skin is changing colour. She is glowing, a luminous blue. I catch my reflection in the water. So this is who I am. My eyes are yellow. The iris is not round but rectangular. Nausea and fear grip me when I reach down and realise there are tentacles where my feet were. Eight slimy tentacles. I don't have to count them because I can feel each one moving me further into the sea. Nkaiseng's little tentacles grab onto my arm.

Ndumiso's arms were trying to push me away but he couldn't move. He was scared. I could hear him screaming inside. The tentacles were twisted around his torso. I didn't mean to hurt him. It didn't even occur to me that I was squeezing him to death. How could I have known that I was transforming into something so powerful? We were both suspended in a moment of instinct. His was to run away. Mine was to lay still in shock. The bottom half of me, that I didn't even realise was there, had a different reaction. I was trying to push myself up when a tentacle wrapped itself around my limp wrist. I screamed. When I realised that the tentacles came from beneath my khanga, I looked at Ndumiso. Foaming at the mouth and choking on blood, only his eyes were moving. The tentacles were attached to me but I didn't know how to control them. I wasn't breathing, stomach and tentacles in knots. My body and the thing that was trying to take over were not in sync. I could feel Ndumiso's heartbeat through the tentacles; it was slowing. 'No,' my voice fell. In that moment all I could hear was Ndumiso's fading breathing. It wasn't supposed to be like this.

'This is who we are,' Koko began.

I tried to stifle a sob. My grandmother was telling me that the women in my family were believed to be cursed. 'I didn't believe it myself until I had Lipuo. The other things that happened, when I was a teenager, scared me. I was always a girl with no friends. It was easier to convince myself that I had imagined or dreamed the strange things that happened to me. A secret becomes harder to keep when there are other people involved. Did you ever wonder why our family has only women?' Koko's words didn't make sense to me. 'Our whole family. We only give birth to women. Not many. Just one.' Koko didn't have any siblings, neither did her mother, or mine, for that matter. 'There are many stories about us. I've only heard them from other people who are not my mother. All I know is that the women in our family always used to live near the sea, rivers and lakes. Do you know why, Manoka?' My grandmother was folding and unfolding the hem of her dress. She reached up and flattened her hair. 'Because we are ...' I didn't complete the sentence because Ndumiso's scared face came back to me. 'Yes. Yes, we are. When I gave birth to Lipuo, my mother never left my side. But that's what mothers do. They stay with their daughters and help them become mothers. She insisted on giving her a bath inside our house, never outside, no matter how hot it was.' Our eyes met and she answered the question I didn't have to ask. 'One day my mother asked me to join her as she gave Lipuo a bath. There in the water, my baby changed before my eyes.' My stomach was in knots again. 'Was she like me?' 'Yes and no. We all take on different shapes. You have those long things.' Koko smiled. 'Bath time was challenging with you.'

'Nkaiseng? What does she …'

'She is a little like you but hers sting.' I tried to imagine my small baby all soft and cuddly but with tentacles, like a jellyfish, below the waist. 'I try to immerse her in water as little as possible,' Koko said, shaking her head.

'Why did I stop being that way?'

'It must be the breastfeeding. While mother and child are connected they are …'

'Mermaids?'

'I'm not sure if you can call us that but … Listen to me. You can go away and learn our history and be safe from this world.'

'Where would I go?'

Koko didn't have to answer. The answer was always somewhere in my heart. I would have to run away … Into the water.

Up to my chest in water, Nkaiseng a short distance in front of me and Koko behind me on the beach, I tried not to cry. My grandmother was standing on the shore. She couldn't come with us. 'Not until the end,' she said. 'Women like us only have three chances to live where we come from: when we are born, while we're breastfeeding or being breastfed, and when we die. It won't be too long now, my child.'

Koko said she would find her way back to the water and we would all be together soon.

'My mother?' I don't even know why I asked that, Lipuo was so rarely on my mind.

'I was once told that mothers know when their daughters are to return. She may be waiting for you inside our world.'

Our world. That is where I was headed. Panic returns when I realise Nkaiseng has disappeared under the water. I turn around, wave goodbye to Koko and use the bottom half of my body to pull myself beneath the water. A searing pain cuts into my sides. My mouth fills with water as I try to scream. I am going to drown. I have never been underwater. But the water doesn't fill my lungs. It feels cold inside my chest and then it passes through the sides of my T-shirt. One tentacle reaches for Nkaiseng, still a cautious baby, who is not too far away, and my right hand feels under my shirt. Between the bones of my ribs are slits. Open flesh that looks like gills. A film of skin closes over my eyes and the water stops burning them. We are finally submerged, a baby and her mother underwater. Nkaiseng doesn't swim as well as I do. I keep one tentacle around her waist and look around us. It's still too dark to see much. As we get lower I spot something I recognise: red takkies. It is Ndumiso — lifeless. A second tentacle reaches for him. His body weighs me down a bit but I remember Koko's words: 'Accidents happen when a cursed woman loves a man. If he dies in water, you can get him back. Not the same as before but he will understand you better. That's what I've heard. Maybe there's some truth in it.'

I hope he does. Maybe at the bottom, we will finally be free. Together.

Ghost Strain N

Koketso may have been the first to notice and it hurt him physically. His stomach ached for days when the size and shape of the problem became evident. How could the neighbourhood not realise what was happening? If people who lived close enough to smell each other's dinners couldn't see it, what about those who didn't know the names of their neighbours? Being a young person whose observations and opinions were not valued, Koketso knew nobody would believe him. By the time official announcements had been made, hearts had been eaten and whole neighbourhoods evacuated. You see, a major event is really just a string of small, overlooked events holding hands. One of the little hands was when Koketso stopped using adjectives. How could he possibly describe anything when the world around him had lost its colour?

Steven was the Colour, ever since they were kids; Koketso drew the lines and saw the bigger picture but Steven always added the colour and purpose. Girls were the bright Saffron of their afternoons but also the Grey of their rejection. Weekends with Steven were Purple – either Royal or a messy Mulberry stain. They both added something to each other's lives. Before he met Koketso, Steven was just floating and rarely feeling; as soon as they became friends, he started to like the warmth of the feelings he sometimes caught. Aimless Saturday afternoons became an opportunity for Koketso to listen to Steven talking to people who passed by his uncle's house: 'Mtshepana, you're still wearing those fake shoes? You're letting the neighbourhood down, wena. This is why the boys in this neighbourhood don't have girlfriends. Usifakela is'nyama, Tshepo.' Many people commented that they had never seen Koketso laugh before Steven came into his life.

Because they attended different schools, Koketso found that his hours at school remained anaemic, and Steven found that he was followed by a relentless emptiness to every class. Every few months Steven found a new hobby for them to take up. The one that Koketso could never get into was graffiti; the smell of the spray paint made him dizzy and he didn't think he had a creative bone in his body. He'd just watch Steven paint everything from walls of abandoned buildings to portaloos and sometimes cars. The source of the spray paint also made Koketso nervous: Steven mumbled something about a friend who knew about his passion.

Trainsurfing was by far the most exciting (and stupidly dangerous) hobby that Steven introduced. Once a week they would take a train instead of a taxi home from school. Once inside, they would slide out of the windows onto the top of the train. Koketso only took part because he had worked out that the likelihood of them being electrocuted was low, given the slow speed of the train on their way home. Still, it was thrilling for Koketso to watch his friend dance on top of the moving train; it made him feel alive. Isn't that why we are alive, to feel alive? was what he thought, when his mother threatened to kill him herself rather than have to collect his charred corpse because he was trainsurfing.

They became friends in the way men and boys do: proximity. Steven moved in next door when Koketso was already an outsider both at school and in the neighbourhood. Unfamiliar with the hierarchy of their one tiny street with no tarred surface or streetlights, Steven dared to speak to the invisible boy. Together they carved their own place in the claustrophobic living space, chased girls who bared their teeth in fear, exchanged clips of comedians on their phones and occasionally shared food when one or the other hadn't eaten for a few days. Steven had the taste buds of a culinary genius when it came to improvising and matching flavours. He could make magic out of a can of pilchards, toasted bread, morogo and onions (that were nearly dustbin suitable). Koketso, on the other hand, was only good at observing, being a companion and occasional comic relief. He had spent enough time by himself to become a master of observation and entertaining himself.

High school did nothing to prepare them for a life burdened with complications. Koketso's complication was that he couldn't afford to study further, so he started working at a funeral home. A quiet young man with big, sympathetic eyes, he found the perfect use for his kind face. When grieving families saw him walking around the funeral home, they relaxed a little. They mistook his silence for respect and his disinterest for awareness of how difficult the loved one's death was for them.

Steven found himself dealing with a complication that had become common in his neighbourhood: dreams deferred and idle days. He had once told his uncle that he had dreams of being a chef. The callous laughter that followed informed him that his dreams should become unvoiced. Koketso tiptoed around the dead while his best friend walked loudly among those who wanted to die.

You would think that the nation would have sat up when its young people lost their ability to stand up straight or speak. If nothing else, people who are harassed by life have a wry sense of humour, because they would eventually call these vacant young people 'Ghosts'. Nothing happened as these Ghosts were overtaking corners of the townships. Saliva dripped from their mouths as their muscles relaxed, eyes half shut, some bent over in the kind of ecstasy and agony oblivion brings. When the Ghosts eventually came to Koketso's part of town, he was shocked into silence. He periodically wrote obituaries, when he wasn't getting tea for bereaved families, driving the hearse or arguing with the mortician. The government mortuary was inept and frequently they would give Koketso the wrong corpse. At least twice a week he could be seen running into the mortuary shouting, 'Aaaargha

Jerry, man! Kanti die man doesn't know what he's doing!' It was on one of those afternoons, when Koketso was heading back to an inconsolable family with the correct corpse, that he noticed a Ghost at the traffic lights.

The Ghost was wearing a brown jersey, jeans that needed a wash and tattered shoes (Ghosts sometimes sell their expensive takkies in exchange for oblivion). His right arm was hooked around a pole, holding up the rest of the body. The Ghost was not slumped over or falling, but graciously suspended in a moment of sliding down the pole, except that his knees had locked and he looked like a life-sized photograph frozen in that position. There was nothing in his eyes, nothing but oblivion. Drool fell from his mouth, just missing the tattered shoes that he had probably stolen from another Ghost. People were flying, oblivious, past the Ghost suspended in time. Nobody noticed it until a small girl with a big dog poked him with a stick in the way curious children think is appropriate; she tried to say something to him and then ran after her dog that was attempting to cross the busy street.

Koketso decided to fast for a week. Children with religious parents are often breastfed the faith and its rituals or, like Koketso, they find refuge in the rituals and not the God. When there wasn't enough food for all her children, his mother would fast and pray. From a young age, Koketso learned to listen to his stomach; when anything bothered him he would fast the way he had always seen his mother do. She fussed over him, because she hated that he was unsettled. It was a mood she knew all too well; even when he was a baby, she could tell just by looking at him that it would rain with thunder and lightning. No matter how bright the day started out, her son's face was the only forecast she trusted. When a particularly unpleasant relative was about to surprise them with an unwanted visit, Koketso would suddenly refuse food. On those days, his mother would throw him on her back, lock up the house and go visit a friend. Only when he cried, a hungry cry, would she know that it was safe to go home.

Because of Koketso's job, the two friends hadn't seen each other in weeks – which is an eternity for boys who grew up together in spite of what the elements wanted. Missing Steven, Koketso went looking for his friend. Home was the obvious first choice; if not there then probably on the streets surrounding the place where he laid his head down. Not finding him on a Friday afternoon didn't worry Koketso – Steven enjoyed partying in other neighbourhoods; the girls there were less likely to have run into his ex-girlfriends or know that he only splurged on drinks when his uncle's disability grant had come in. Saturday was when Koketso was busiest at work; there were always back-to-back funerals. He got home exhausted and slept the day away. Sunday was busy until lunchtime and he was certain that Steven would either wait for him outside the funeral home or show up for lunch at his house. The Sunday lunch appearances were becoming regular – Koketso would watch his friend eat like a man with multiple stomachs. His eyes were in a perpetual state of waking up, turned down and glassy. Steven's uncle was only worried because he didn't like to be alone and Steven hadn't been home for two weeks.

The next day at work, Koketso heard Mamokgethi, his boss, talking to Jerry. 'Is it true, Jerry?'

'I saw it for myself. Her heart was ripped out and covered in bite marks.'

'What is the world coming to? Modimo!'

'I don't know but this is gruesome.'

Koketso entered the kitchen where the two gossips stood holding cups of coffee. Jerry's hand was resting on top of Mamokgethi's; they quickly moved away from each other. 'Koketso, hey man!'

'Jerry. I'm coming to do a pick-up, please make sure it's the right one.'

Jerry chuckled and nodded but he was obviously annoyed.

Whispers about hearts being torn out of people continued and they got louder. In churches, shebeens, kitchens and bedrooms, that is what people were talking about. Ghosts colonised street corners and the fences of the corner houses. Koketso fainted at work (a promise to God to stop eating until Steven was found) and was sent home. He had resorted to bargaining with a god he didn't really believe in. A little bit of soup and bread did him some good but he still felt as though something horrible was coming – his stomach was screaming danger. Huddled at the kitchen table, he looked at his mother and siblings. He knew they had to go; the township was never safe but now it was unquestionably dangerous. After dinner Koketso asked his mother to take his younger siblings and go visit his grandmother.

'Why?'

'It's school holidays and I've been saving up money for you guys to go.' That wasn't exactly a lie – he had been saving up money but it was for extending their tiny house so his siblings could have their own room, instead of sleeping on the floor of his.

'Are you coming?'

'No. I have to work. Buy the tickets tomorrow and go surprise your family. You always talk about how much you miss home.'

'It has been five years since I've seen my mother and brother.' His mother blinked away tears, tilted her head to one side and said, 'You're such a kind boy.'

By the time national newspapers, radio stations and TV stations were covering the 'outbreak' it was too late for many. It happened so fast; in less than two weeks whole neighbourhoods were emptied, many hearts extracted and countless Ghosts burned, because mob justice knows no sentimentality. The burning of Ghosts began in townships because the illness was euphemised in the suburbs. Even those with fancy houses, money, and gentle words like 'euthanasia' couldn't escape the Ghosts. The funeral home was busier than ever and sometimes Koketso didn't even know whether he was comforting the right family. It didn't matter because they were all shocked and, most of all, frightened. He sent his mother a quick and concise message after every one of the funerals: *Still safe. Work busy. Miss U guys.*

Koketso had just come home from work when he heard a commotion outside. There was a group gathering in the street outside his bedroom window. He had become numb in the days that lacked colour or a sighting of Steven. The group was hiding or blocking someone with the circle that their bodies created. There was yelling, profanities, people crying and other noises Koketso couldn't or wouldn't identify. Somewhere in the back of his mind, he knew that Steven would be next. Could he live with knowing that he did nothing to save his only friend? Was Steven so far gone that some other group of frightened, angry people would see fit to kill him, rather than let him eat the hearts of people? He didn't come to any satisfactory conclusion but he knew what had to be done, and packed a bag. Filled it in a hurry with knives, a knobkerrie, his mother's church shawl, toilet paper, other things he thought would be important, and all the canned food he could find.

Mamokgethi trusted him with the keys to the hearse because she thought he was too dull to do anything dangerous or expensive. He once overheard her telling the receptionist that he was too mild. 'He's so mild. I know I should be grateful because these other kids out there are killing themselves and others, but yoo ha ah, what a dull boy!'

Being dull finally paid off, Koketso thought, as he drove in whatever direction he imagined might lead him to Steven. 'Just look for the most colourful street, that's where he will be,' Koketso kept telling himself. He hoped that Jerry and his boss would forgive him for stealing some equipment from the mortuary: the extreme state of affairs required a little bit of 'not dull' behaviour from him. A quarter of the neighbourhood had already left; there was not enough attachment to material things that would make them risk losing their children. Koketso's own mother was very worried about him. She made him promise that he would pack up a few things and join them at her brother's house further inland. He lied, and she let him. Fear and trauma make you accept little lies to silence the truth because when the truth is young people breaking into homes, tearing hearts out of people's chests and eating them, anything is better than admitting that life will never be the same. Even the police denied that Ghosts were impervious to bullets, the way they just kept walking – not even stumbling when hit – in search of drugs, or hearts, and sometimes both. They never attacked each other, though. Their appetite was for those who were not lost.

Steven, even as a living-dead thing, still seemed like he was emitting neon fumes. Koketso found him after a few hours of searching.

He was hiding in a bush, eating something stringy and bloody. It was the luminous bush, in front of an unremarkable grey house, that acted like a magnet to Koketso. He followed the cloud of colour behind the bush and his heart leapt. At first, it seemed like Steven recognised his own name; he looked up at his friend and attempted to stand. Then something wild flashed across his face as he stumbled back, his manic eyes moving from Koketso to his own hands. A searing rage launched his body forward, his hands clawing at the chest of the person he once considered a brother. Koketso didn't run or back away; he took the silver chain he had stolen off a long-gone neighbour's gate and wrapped it around the unusually strong Ghost formerly known as Steven. They struggled for a few minutes but when Koketso tightened the chain around the Ghost's chest, it was easier to drag him to the back of the hearse. The angry screams of Ghost Steven, the clattering of chains and shoes and skin scraping on the gravel, drew the attention of people in a house nearby. 'Hey! Vha khou ita mini?' one of the people from the house shouted, wanting to know what was going on. Koketso didn't take his eyes off what he was doing; heaving a living body into a coffin was much more difficult than he'd thought. But he didn't give up. The Steven he knew seemed to be hiding somewhere behind the eyes of the Ghost in the coffin.

A group of people was now walking towards him. 'Hey! Hey wena mfana! Are you deaf? What are doing here? It must be one of those Nyaope dealers.'

Koketso didn't wait to see what those people would do to a person they suspected of being a drug dealer in a time of Ghosts, paranoia and fear.

Nyaope was just another name for an opportunist. Where society left a gap, this opportunist took over. It was an opportunist that slipped into your hand, lied to your heart and ate your brain. Scientists were calling it a virus; Koketso didn't believe that — he had seen with his own eyes its genesis. In just a few months things had fallen apart all over the world. Many people had died — their corpses quickly incinerated because films and TV shows taught us that the undead could create more undead. There were reports of increasing numbers of Ghosts cropping up all over the world; doctors and scientists still didn't know how the 'virus' was spreading or if it was even possible to cure it. There were different strains of virus and each one had a different effect on the Ghosts and the neighbourhoods that ignored or housed them. The one Koketso was dealing with was known as Ghost Strain N. 'Ghost' because those who had it were virtually dead before they had it — broken people who turned to a life of oblivion and homelessness even when they had places to lay their heads at night. 'N' because in his neighbourhood it was Nyaope that had sustained the Ghosts; it kept them alive and in search of the next fall down a bottomless pit, until the high ended and yanked them back into a world they hated. Nyaope was particularly unforgiving because it could be a mixture of almost anything and heroin. Ghost Strain T in the Western Cape made the Ghost chew the hands and arms off people. T was for Tik. Ghost Strain W hit farm workers on Wine farms where Ghosts ripped the throats out of people and ate them. Koketso thought a lot about the different strains and what drove Ghosts to attack certain body parts and not others. He finally decided that Strain W made Ghosts rip out the oesophagus from people because they had wine poured down their throats instead of being compensated and invested in by those who profited from their labour.

The Ghost Virus was quick, violent and efficient. Hospitals could not keep up with the many people who were brought in; some died where they fell and the army was left to identify and dispose of the dead. Very soon the country became a Ghost Town where most of what made people feel secure, fell away. There were no more jobs to wake up for, nor was there civility or respect for the property of others. There was no longer a threat of hell, or suffering afterlife, if they didn't love their neighbour. Hell visiting Earth had stripped away the good nature they had always assumed was inherent. Koketso held on to hope and everything he had ever seen in B-Grade movies about an unlikely hero making it to the end in one piece. He breathed in hope that fuelled a belief that his family was safe; there was no way of communicating with them but hope never relied on evidence. Many years of watching B-Grade (and sometimes C-Grade) action films prepared him for the kind of athleticism and quick thinking that would keep him alive. Love made him carry his best friend, the only person who ever made him want to be better, in a coffin in the backs of various stolen cars.

All his life, Koketso wanted to travel and see more of his own country and places that were unfamiliar. He got his wish. For months he kept stealing SUVs and trucks that had enough space to carry a coffin. It was after a month of this that he finally heard Steven say something. Koketso had found a food-canning factory. It looked like a place that had been interrupted during lunchtime − empty but thick with the promise of returning workers. It took two hours to find food because the place had been recently scouted. This was something he was getting used to, finding empty places robbed of anything useful. Everything was being repurposed. He chuckled when he was scouting for houses and saw one with all the glass taken out of the window panes.

After packing into the car as much canned food as he could find in the factory, he drove on until he spotted an abandoned farmhouse. They stayed in one of the worker's quarters at the back of the property, to avoid being spotted from the road. The world fell silent and Koketso saw hardly any people; when he did, it was on the road and he avoided eye contact with the faces in the passing vehicles. Once, he thought he heard voices coming from a house he was about to scout. The trouble of killing a Ghost wasn't worth it, so he moved on to another house.

Over time, houses were reverting back to nature. Those who once lived in them could never have imagined their homes covered by curtains of grass and vines. Pavements were one-third concrete and two-thirds whatever was being suppressed beneath it. Nature was no longer something confined to game farms or manicured to look acceptable. Koketso realised this when he saw a hippo taking a leisurely stroll in a street he was driving along. 'Those damn animal rights activists HAD to release all the animals on game farms and in zoos,' Koketso said to himself, equally annoyed and amused. The hair on Koketso's head grew as wild and thick as the vegetation he saw. His mother had always insisted on short hair because only 'MaRasta and these boys who like drugs' had long hair. Some neighbourhoods had water, others didn't. Electricity was a luxury that Koketso had never really become accustomed to anyway, so he always had a Primus stove in the back of the car. He bathed in cold water and only used paraffin for the stove if there was nowhere to make a fire.

Koketso didn't like to leave Steven in the coffin all day but often it was a necessity. He had tried driving with him in the passenger seat but that ended up with Koketso being bitten by Steven, and a few scratches on the side of the car. Some nights he would have to leave his best friend locked up in the coffin, if he was driving through the night. On those nights his stomach would ache and Koketso would just keep driving until he could breathe again. At the back of the farmhouse, he lit a fire and propped Steven up against a tree. The shock of his friend not dying from starvation never went away. 'Aaah mara wena, san. You're really gonna make me carry you in a coffin with me for the rest of my life?' Koketso laughed like he was having a conversation with a responsive person. Steven just managed to grunt and sway a little.

Every night was like that – a soliloquy peppered with hope but never a response from Steven.

The loneliness had turned Koketso into a person who gave running commentary on his every move. His invisible audience was a constant companion, so even when Steven did mutter something, it was missed. Koketso was rubbing oil on vegetarian sausages and giving his best TV Chef impression: 'Now I picked these sausages because the meat ones were putrid and these ones seemed to be okay. Nyaope boys have turned us into vegetarians; health conscious and on the run. Rub oil on the sausage, like so. Drizzle just a little ...' Koketso stopped and looked at Steven. It had finally happened – he'd known it was just a matter of time until the things inside his mind jumped out into the material world and he finally lost his fragile grip on reality. Steven's vacant eyes were focused on the stars above them. Koketso opened his mouth to say something else when he heard a mumble coming from where Steven was sitting: 'Heh monna, are you speaking?'

The words he heard left Koketso in tears; the words were mashed up in an undead mouth, but he heard them. He dropped his vegetarian sausages and fell off the bunk stool he was perched on. Steven stared vacantly at the scene in front of him. Three words inspired hope and desperation: 'O senya oil.' It was nothing

44

profound or even remotely touching. Steven, the gifted culinary genius, scolded his friend for wasting grapeseed oil. Somewhere inside the Ghost was a stubborn young man who fought the rot and emptiness, just to stop the wasting of grapeseed oil. Koketso crouched in front of the swaying shell of the person that was his friend and touched his hand. 'Okay, Gordon Ramsay wase kasi. I'm gonna keep cooking bad food until you get better.' With that, he sat back on the bunk stool, picked up the sausages from the floor, dusted them off and held them over the fire with braai tongs. The sausages were oily but tasted like they had expired only in theory. 'Maybe I should have listened to you about the oil, but I doubt anything could make this crap taste good.' Steven grunted, to which Koketso answered, 'Ja okay. Maybe I should have just had peanut butter on a spoon. I'm not the cook here. You are.' His lonely voice tapered off into the starry night until all that was left was the sound of crickets and frogs.

Koketso knew that he was the first to notice the Ghosts. His stomach still ached when the pressure of living among them grew overwhelming. Trust died when the president dispatched the army to catch and 'cure' (a euphemism for incinerating Ghosts). Small human rights groups protested the killing of people just because they were ill, and innocent victims died in the crossfire. People hiding in their own homes were mistaken for Ghosts. TV stations stopped broadcasting and radio stations played emergency automated playlists until one day there was nothing on radio. Koketso was now on the run with his Ghost friend – he was not ready to give up on Steven. They avoided strangers, the army and houses that could be seen from the road. The world was grey for some but for Koketso the sky was a sweet Azure, and even the dying grass in front of the abandoned mansions was Mellow Yellow. Some days when Steven seemed to be sleeping, the colours faded but it didn't bother Koketso because he was never vibrant to begin with. Somewhere inside the Ghost mind, he knew Steven was trapped. At least that's what he wanted to believe because the places where Steven had bitten him were beginning to itch a little. He had been bitten when he first tied Steven up and a few times after that when he carried him out of the coffin and into the moonlight. The skin around the bite marks was turning Mauve with a Green tinge to the outlines. The colours glowed a little in the dark and Koketso liked it, even against his better judgement. He looked up at Steven and swore he saw a crooked, tired smile on his grey, sunken-in face.

The Parlemo

On a corner, now named for two activists who are neither Mandela nor Biko, where two apartheid-era presidents used to meet, a few kilometres away from the headquarters of the old stock exchange, is a shop with two names. Those who call it The Parlemo expect you to know about a war, and about Italian Prisoners of War in South Africa. This information is vital because it leads us to the (often bungled) story of a man named Marcello who escaped from a POW camp and eventually ended up in the Transvaal. The Parlemo crowd simply refuses to acknowledge its new name: Café Ferdi. According to them, Marcello (the son, not the POW) is the only owner they acknowledge. The Parlemo crowd has never owned a cellphone but they all possess one bought by an overbearing grandchild or great grandchild. They dress up to go to 'the shops' and think it's a shame the 'old neighbourhood' is gone.

The Parlemo is a little shop that is very easy to miss. You must not judge yourself harshly for not seeing one of the oldest buildings on the block. You're probably oblivious to things outside your areas of interest and, if we're being quite honest, the shop doesn't want to be seen. It doesn't have anything you've lost or want to remember. And it has a way of camouflaging itself – it has done this for many years. Even during 'the bad old days' the police could never see that little 'kafee' where people of different races dared to sit down next to each other and enjoy food made by Manini, the chef who made whatever her heart desired for the customers. She and Marcello, the owner, worked at The Parlemo until their grandchildren took over from them. That's the way things are, and always have been, at The Parlemo: unorthodox and unchanged. Except, of course, that it's now called Café Ferdi.

Brooke is standing outside Café Ferdi, biting her bottom lip and trying to decide if she's ready for what awaits her inside. Out comes Ta James, a retired playboy; he's seen something in there that has annoyed him. 'Aaaagh, kanti why does this thing always come up? Were there no good times?'

Brooke giggles because she can guess why Ta James is so upset. Ten years ago he slept with his wife's sister and she confronted him inside Café Ferdi. It's a memory that haunts him mostly when he goes in to buy the same wine that he used to charm both sisters with. Calling it 'wine' is generous but that's what most patrons buy when former 'town shebeens' are littered with children who play at poverty by dressing like homeless people. That's what freedom is, right? 'Nelson Mandela did not die for us to be repressed' – that's what Brooke once heard the children born after freedom exclaim at a bar. Irony and humour is not their strong point. Cannibalism is, though. They're going to consume this whole place and spit it out like the spoiled brats that they are, thought Brooke.

New ambition was eating old comforts; new bricks over old foundations and facelifts were the order of the day. Beneath the buildings, stuck in the concrete, was the blood and sweat of those who had built the city. Beneath their sweat lay the limbs and dreams of those who were digging the core of the earth on the promise of a better life (it never materialised). What were once the offices of a (liberal or communist, depending on your politics) newspaper had become a gym filled with people who cycled to work. The cycling lanes were painted over streets that had absorbed the blood of the journalists who were often harassed by a paranoid system with overzealous policemen. Red Cappuccinos replaced the decades-old smell of sorghum beer brewed in a backroom that was now a tiny coffee shop featured in the *New York Times*. Under the grey paint, new bricks, repurposed school desks, copper fittings and overpriced shoes are vaults of history – in all its agony and joy.

Brooke, named after her mother's favourite soapie character, lived in the city centre after white flight. It was a dark time for those who 'ran' from Swart Gevaar-inspired fantasies. Most moved back to their 'mother countries' or the suburbs (a different kind of motherland), except for Ferdinando – a Portuguese man who sold the best peri-peri chicken and chips from his small café. The current owner is a young guy who seems generally uninterested in everything except Brooke. When she enters the store, he secretly hopes that she encounters happier times. He can see her hesitating outside but the rules of being a vault keeper require that he mind the vault he's in charge of and nothing else. Most of the patrons call him Thoko – which is a girl's name and a shortened version of his name, Thokozane, which is not even his real name because he's from Rwanda, but that's what he chooses to call himself and everybody minds his or her own business.

Brooke stepped inside knowing that by setting foot in the shop, she was allowing it to pickpocket her mind. Whenever you stepped into Café Ferdi, you were agreeing to have some of your memories stolen. The only way to access those memories was to come back and have them play out like a movie in front of you. Terms and conditions apply. That's why Ta James was so upset. He had gone in to get his favourite (cheap) wine and ended up watching his humiliating afternoon of scandal. Where his wife and sister-in-law threw bottles of the wine at him and called him a dog. Nobody can say why the sisters didn't turn on each other or why they should have, but it was a huge surprise for all those present. Usually infidelity was the problem of the main and the mistress. They tore at each other's faces and hair in front of everyone while the object of their affection learned nothing.

Brooke was there to learn something she had forgotten about Sidwell. The message he sent her last week was puzzling: *U R the one for me. Just say da word and I will leave her. Ur da 1 4 me.* The break-up was a long time coming but the reason for it was blurry which meant it was stuck at Café Ferdi. Brooke agonised over it for weeks because she knew that she would be giving up another memory in order to access the one she desperately needed. She had not responded to Sidwell and he had started calling her at least once a day, calls she didn't answer, during his lunch break at work; Brooke was neither moved nor concerned. How difficult was it to call someone during your lunch break at the call centre?

Thoko gave her a head nod and she winked at him. 'Cigarettes?' he asked. 'Not today, babe. Just here for … uhm milk.' Thoko sighed and said, 'You know where to find it. Always in the same place.' Café Ferdi should have been a liquor store because it had a walk-in fridge but instead of all the beer and ciders you could think of, there was fresh produce. Brooke gave a deep sigh and opened the fridge. Instead of a cold breeze, she was greeted by a warm summer one. She was tempted to take her poncho off but she resisted. Inside the fridge was the facade of a theatre where she was going to star in her first play. She watched a younger (her hair hadn't yet grown into a difficult-to-style afro) version of herself and Sidwell sitting on the stairs outside the Windybrow Theatre in downtown Johannesburg. She was wearing harem pants and a red T-shirt with Robert Sobukwe's face on it. Sobukwe was smiling and had a pipe hanging from his mouth. In contrast, Brooke was frowning. Sidwell was staring at his shoes and smoking a cigarette. 'What do you mean?'

'I just mean you're not very good,' Sidwell said, blowing out a cloud of smoke while talking.

'Not good at acting?' Brooke asked, tugging at Sobukwe uncomfortably.

'Babe, we all have our things and I think you should stick to yours.'

'What's my thing, Sidwell?'

'Your stats at the call centre are good and you're earning decent money.'

'But why can't I do both?' Brooke asked, a little wounded.

Sidwell smiled but she missed it because he turned his face away from her. 'Because you're only good at one.'

'I got a great review in the *Sowetan*. The critic said I was ...'

'Babe, *Sowetan* is a rag. Just forget this.'

Brooke shoved her box of cigarettes in her harem pants and stood up. 'I'm sorry you feel that way. I'm gonna keep doing this. Maybe WE are not meant to be.'

The words landed hard on him but he played it cool and laughed. 'Your loss, Brooke.'

She walked towards the theatre and he stubbed his cigarette

out violently and muttered awful words about a woman he claimed to love.

When they first met, Sidwell was an aspiring music producer, producing for small-time rappers who spammed people with SoundCloud links to their bland lyrics about fake lives, whereas all of Brooke's auditions were unsuccessful. Brooke was practising lines for a small play when they met. 'Poetry?' Sidwell asked, sitting down next to her and drowning his slap chips with tomato sauce and mayonnaise. Brooke shook her head, 'Play. Audition this weekend.' He offered to read over lines with her; she in turn listened to him dreaming about one of his songs making it onto national radio stations. Tenderness was not what made Brooke go on a first date with him – it was the eyes. Sidwell always looked at her when he spoke to her; it made him seem sincere. Even when he grew frustrated with not getting a big break, Brooke stayed because he never took his eyes off her ... until the night of her big play.

Brooke was back in the fridge. 'Tjeeer! So fucking jealous. Jealous fuck!' she shouted and grabbed a carton of milk that she didn't even need because she was lactose intolerant. Thoko offered her free gum and a weak smile. 'Sure, mf'ethu,' she said.

'How's your mother?' Thoko asked softly.

'The same ... dementia is awful but you would know because ...' Brooke stretched her hands out, indicating the store. Thoko sighed and gave her change. He wished that the memory she had just accessed was a happy one, even though she was likely to forget it within ten minutes of leaving the shop. Being a Vault Keeper was supposed to be easy, but people were so attractive in their warmth, stupidity and humanity. Café Ferdi was just another vault – one of many around the world. Humankind was prone to forgetting the big things: wars, theft and other horrors. It is the human condition. There are certain places, all around the world, that have been neglected; this neglect changes the way history is shaped, so the soil, bricks and cement turn themselves into a vault. Vault Keepers are born to their role and sent on assignment away from their homes. The Vault Keepers' League is perhaps the most well-hidden group in the world. It is made up of people from all over the world, existing in hidden buildings and working easily forgotten jobs. They guard the vaults and leave when the next assignment requires them. Vault Keepers have been around for as long as cities and villages have been witness to human pain and kindness.

There are many stories about how The Parlemo came to be, the most popular one being about a young man,

Something-something Marcello, who arrived in South Africa as a Prisoner of War in 1941. The people who tell this story overlook the war and how a POW moved from Natal to Transvaal. They really want to get to the part of the story that is fun to say: 'The man's surname was Marcello, he was from Parlemo, and so he decreed that every son born in his family would be named Marcello from Parlemo. The POW wanted his descendants never to forget who they are and where they come from. And so there was one Marcello from Parlemo and another and another.' While the language of Parlemo still made curious music with the newly acquired English – placing emphasis on the wrong syllables – a Marcello opened a store in what is now Johannesburg city centre.

On a corner, now named for two activists who are neither Mandela nor Biko, where two apartheid-era presidents used to meet, a few kilometres away from the headquarters of the old stock exchange, is a shop with two names. Outside this shop, Café Ferdi, is a girl named Brooke, after her mother's favourite character in a long-running American soapie. She has just spoken on the phone with her mother's caregiver – who wanted to find out if she could label the pre-packed meals by the day. Brooke is staring at her phone and a memory is already fading from her mind. She walks away from the shop that remains hidden to many and she begins to type a reply to a message from a boy named Sidwell: *Ok. Let's meet 2moro. Missed U 2. On my way to rehearsal. Luv U always.*

Untitled i

Bonolo was taking washing off the line when the sky suddenly looked like it was going to open up and pour. There was Kamo's uniform that needed to be ironed before she got supper ready. Summer was always Bonolo's favourite season. The fruit was better, nights were shorter – but she wasn't crazy about how quickly rainclouds could gather and ruin a perfectly productive laundry day.

Rhulani, the woman who was renting space in their backyard, where she'd built a shack, was sitting on the stoep peeling potatoes. The loose peels were falling into the dip of her skirt and the peeled potatoes into a round dish filled with water by her feet. She and Bonolo were talking about something insignificant but amusing when Rhulani suddenly looked up and gasped. The sun had dimmed; quite suddenly the daylight turned from grey to the colour of the hour before children are called in because the streetlights are on. The sun was definitely still in the sky, but angry clouds that looked like a frustrated artist's splashes of paint blocked it. People stood in the streets, looking at the sky with curiosity, which grew into panic when it became apparent that the experts didn't have any answers. *'What good are these bloody smart people if they can never give us answers when we need them?'*

The hour-before-night sky stayed, and people's fear of it dulled after a few weeks. Fear of the unknown is actually a fear of an unknown death by an unknown beast. Nobody seemed to be dying, so they made the best of whatever God/the ancestors had given them. World leaders blamed each other for not being Climate Change Ready and spies gathered information on those who had predicted the sun being upstaged. While the blame game continued, giant floodlights were being put up in major cities, to mimic the daylight. Thieves and lovers used the darkness to their advantage and others turned to humour:

'How can I be late for work if it's always night time?'

'I can't be the only one who is constantly in the mood, right? Night time is the right time, phela!'

'Might as well get drunk, wanna rock up to hell properly happy.'

'End of days? For the rest of the world maybe. We are used to disasters here in SA. Just look at our government.'

Bonolo, a light sleeper, woke up because heavy-footed Kamo was up and moving around the house as if in a panic. 'Did you forget to bring the bucket in again?' Bonolo asked sleepily. Using the outside toilet was far too dangerous since the sun had disappeared, so they relied on a bucket. Bringing the bucket in was usually Kamo's duty, which she conveniently forgot most days. Her bladder was also annoyingly busy while others slept.

Kamo didn't answer. Instead, she threw clothes onto the bed and said, 'Get dressed.'

'It's not morning yet. The clocks work just f—'

'Bonolo!'

Kamo was always self-assured; even as a toddler she would push herself up and walk with only one hand pressed against the wall, no fuss and no fear. On her first day of school, she clutched the straps of her oversized bag, got out the taxi and ran to the school gates without looking back. Bonolo cried all the way to

her school because she was worried about her little sister and her
mind had played out all the worst first-school-day possibilities.
Now, just seeing Kamo on the verge of tears told Bonolo that
something was very wrong.

'What's happening?'

'I'll tell you later but right now we have to leave.'

'Leave? And go where? Why?'

Kamo pulled a suitcase out from under the bed – the suitcase
their mother had bought for the day that one of them finally
went on holiday. 'Somewhere nice where there is a beach,' she'd
said mischievously, when her daughters looked at her in puz-
zlement. Kamo threw some of Bonolo's things into it – many
dresses, the few pairs of jeans she owned, a Sesotho Bible that had
belonged to their mother's aunt, textbooks from the university
and only her 'good' underwear.

Now fully awake, Bonolo got up and peered into the suitcase
as if she hadn't just seen what was thrown into it.

'What is happening?' She hated the whine in her voice so she
cleared it from her throat.

'Please, just trust me. It has to do with the sun. Get dressed,'
Kamo said, fully dressed herself.

Bonolo hadn't yet decided if she was leaving or not but she

threw on the clothes that she had been wearing the previous day. When she picked up her sandals, Kamo snatched them out of her hand and instead gave her the green boots she hardly ever wore. They'd seemed like such a great idea when she saw them in the shop but they made her look like she was in the army (regardless of whether she wore them with a pretty dress or not). 'Where's your stuff?'

Kamo answered the question by picking up a backpack and slinging it over her back. 'In here.'

There was a car waiting for them outside. Bonolo recognised it immediately – it belonged to her mother's ex-employers (Jonty and Annie). How could she forget a car that had so often dropped them off at home after they'd stayed over for dinner at the insistence of Annie? Their mother didn't like it when they did, because for her, it was mixing work and private life and she didn't want her girls getting used to a life that she couldn't afford. She already hated that they thought fast food was a reasonable replacement for food that was already paid for and in the fridge. Most things were a waste of money, according to their mother, Puleng. Her husband thought she was too hard on the girls but he didn't dare say it to her face. Puleng also thought it was inappropriate for them to have a man who was old enough to be their father driving them around like they were rich, spoiled brats. The driver, Meshack, was there now, standing next to the car, smoking a cigarette and looking at his watch. He put the cigarette out when he saw them and made a remark about it being late. Kamo touched his arm and apologised in a sincere way that caught Bonolo off guard: '... had to make sure we had everything we need.' Kamo hated apologising, and yet here she was doing it willingly.

Meshack's eyes didn't meet Bonolo's when she greeted him, making her even more uneasy.

'Listen, Bonolo, we don't have a lot of time so I need you to follow my lead.' Kamo kept talking as they got into the car but none of it made sense to her sister, who was embarrassed that her little sister was in control of a situation that was beginning to frighten her.

'I didn't believe it at first, but this really is it. It's the end. They've been talking about it for weeks. They've known for a long time.'

'What do you mean "the end"? Who is "they"? Where are we going, Kamo?' Bonolo asked, and again she noticed that the driver she knew so well was treating her like a stranger – or a criminal. She got the sense that he viewed her as an intruder.

'Meshack is taking us to a safe place. He has a friend in the military who is going to help.'

Bonolo put her hand on Meshack's shoulder and thanked him; he nodded non-committally and kept his eyes on the road. The longer they were in the car the more she thought about their sleeping neighbours who didn't know that something bad – the thing Kamo called 'the end' – was coming. Panic set in and she cried quietly, trying to hide her tears, not wanting to be the weakest link in an already confusing situation.

The ride to safety was tense. Neither Meshack nor Kamo spoke. Bonolo looked out the window into the familiar darkness. She had been in the back of this very same car a few years ago; on that occasion Jonty was sitting in the front and Meshack had sad eyes. Huddled in the back, she'd kept thinking of the word 'orphan'. That's what she had become after identifying her dead parents. 'Car accident' makes it sound like two cars accidentally spilling a drink on each other. 'Car accident' didn't come close to describing how a taxi had crushed her father's second-hand car. Or the choice the driver had made to overtake a truck on a blind rise at night. She'd silently hoped that this car ride wouldn't end with her crying into her pillow (every night for an entire year).

They arrived at a private airport that she had never heard of – Kamo assured her that it was the right place, with the confidence of someone who regularly flies by private jet to undisclosed locations. Bonolo sometimes ignored how different her and her sister's lives were. At other times the difference jumped out and sat on Bonolo's chest, making it difficult to breathe.

The hangar was bathed in bright lights. Expensive cars were parked outside and she heard announcements being made over a PA system. The voice making the announcements wasn't dispassionate like the ones in the movies. The PA lady's voice was stern; she was obviously Afrikaans speaking but she was trying very hard not to sound Afrikaans. Jonty and his daughter Melanie were waiting at the entrance behind tall private security guys. Jonty said something to one of the guards, who then waved them over.

'Hi. I didn't know you would be here,' Bonolo said, feeling wary when Jonty hugged her. Melanie looked angry but she tried to conceal it with a pathetic smile. She looked past Kamo and acknowledged Meshack with a nod of her head. He closed his eyes briefly, then looked away after she mouthed a sad 'thank you'.

Bonolo felt Kamo's hands on her right elbow then her sister's arms went round her in a tight hug. The hug was too tight, too long and made no sense. 'You'd better go. They only had space for one more. Meshack is waiting for me … Be safe.' No other words were exchanged. Bonolo realised that everybody except her knew what was happening. She closed her eyes and tried to rub the confusion and sleep out of them. Slowly things were starting to come together: Kamo's small bag, Melanie's anger, Meshack's shame – all of it was beginning to make sense. Bonolo shook her head and looked at her little sister, then at Jonty who was always a bad liar. His face told her everything she needed to know.

'No no no no no. Kamo, no!'

'Go, Bonolo!' Her little sister's mouth looked so much like their mother's. Even in the coffin, Puleng was beautiful, her mouth set in a perpetual state of cautious happiness. Kamo opened her mouth but the words got caught in her throat. She tried again, putting on a brave smile. 'You deserve this, Bonolo. If there's a chance for us … I love you. See you soon.'

Melanie finally acknowledged Kamo and they hugged quickly; then Kamo tugged at her backpack and ran back to the car where Meshack was waiting. Jonty wiped his eyes, looked at one of the security guards and nodded. It was the beginning of the end.

Heart in mouth, limbs flailing and words garbled – Bonolo was imploding. The floor beneath her was not steady. One of the private security guys stuck a needle in her neck while another held her arms to her sides. Jonty's arms caught her as she sagged. Melanie groaned. 'This is so unnecessary and dramatic, Dad.'

'It's what Kamo wanted.' His words were sharp but he sounded tired.

Bonolo had never been on a plane but she had seen the interiors of planes in movies and music videos. She knew something was different about this one. It looked like a spaceship that was pretending to be a plane. Bonolo closed her eyes and imagined she could still see Kamo running back to the car – back straight, shoulders back and neck resolute. She never looked back.

Just 14 years old and already a better protector than me, Bonolo thought in a haze of sedatives. Her mouth was moving open and shut like a fish while Annie dressed her in a grey and blue jumpsuit: her least favourite colours. She wanted to tell Annie that she hated those colours – and hated them for abiding by a 14-year-old's decision, but nothing came out of her mouth. 'She's gonna be okay. So are you. You're all right, sweetie,' Annie said. Her mouth was lying and her eyes knew it. When the clouds eclipsed the sun, Bonolo knew deep down that this was bound to end in tears, death or both. A man-shaped blur approached and stood over her. The blur put what looked like a misshapen fishbowl over her head. She felt like she was floating as the blur placed her in an egg-shaped compartment. Her arms, legs and torso were strapped in.

The egg-shaped compartment felt like a fridge. From inside it, she could see outside the spaceship. Slowly she blinked away tears and focused on the sky as they flew into it. The sky was on fire.

The Bad

BnB in Bloem

Busi was growing impatient. Bellinda didn't care – the car needed fixing and hauntings were hardly ever urgent.

'Bloemfontein is a shithole. I wanna be out of here like yesterday.'

'Busi, this is an old car. Calm your tits.'

'Language, Bell.'

'You literally just said "shithole" … and I'm 25!'

'Congratulations. Now watch your fucking mouth.'

It was impossible that their veins contained the same family lines, but they seemed to have the same face. Sometimes people called one's name when looking at the other. When Busisiwe spoke, Bellinda would insert her voice instinctually – creating a harmony that sounded like they had one voice. Their mother, the first of many in a short space of time, only wanted Bellinda. She had a sweet smile, hair in pigtails and appeared to be the perfect little darling for a childless couple. Mother One was already imagining the kind of Sari she would make for Bellinda's wedding day. It was Mam' Gladys who first poured petrol on her dreams. 'Bellinda is … well, she is attached to another little girl here. Perhaps you would like two daughters.'

Not one to let a little thing like fire ruin her dreams, Mrs Naidu refused the extra child and got the daughter she had always dreamed of. Mr Naidu was ambivalent; a little girl was going to make his mother stop nagging about grandchildren – something he was incapable of producing. A boy would have been nice but his wife had made her choice and he wasn't going to argue. The whole parenting thing was not something he'd ever wanted for himself but marriage brings all kinds of good and bad things into one's life.

A charred bedroom carpet and a knife incident lead to Mam' Gladys dropping Busi off, at the Naidu's near-pristine home, for a temporary stay. 'Perhaps that other little girl will help Bellinda settle in. Can we have her for a while, until things settle down?' was what Mrs Naidu said to Mam' Gladys. This was after Bellinda had decided that there was only one person she wanted to talk to: Busi. The temporary stay stretched into a year, by which time Bellinda had destroyed enough of the Naidu's home – more than Mrs Naidu could excuse and Mr Naidu was willing to replace.

'A year was too long, vele,' was what Mam' Gladys said when the girls were marched back into the children's home. She really hadn't expected the girls to stay as long as they did; maybe she had underestimated Mrs Naidu's resolve. Busi just shrugged and Bell ran outside to meet the new children who had arrived at the orphanage while they were with the Naidus.

More mothers and fathers came – mainly for Bellinda, but they always ended up taking both girls. None of the stays lasted longer than three months. Finally Mam' Gladys made a reluctant call to the only couple she knew would know what to do with the girls. The couple, from Port Elizabeth, drove to Durban the following week; Bell and Busi finally had a family ... until the night they went camping as a family and only the girls returned. Mam' Gladys would never forget the look on their teenage faces when they showed up on her doorstep, shaken, injured, bloody and, once again, orphaned.

Port Elizabeth was exactly the kind of quiet both girls needed; a dull place with lacklustre people and no 'great places for kids to hang out'. Bell and Busi were not the kind of children who played well with others and, to their surprise, their new parents didn't push them to. 'We aren't going to put you in a school,' the woman said. She was visibly older than her husband and her accent made Busi giggle. 'You like that?' her husband asked, mildly amused.

For the first few days, the couple kept saying each other's names when talking to the girls. Bell was wary of it because all the other mothers and fathers demanded they be called Mom and Dad almost immediately.

'Abriana, could you please pass me the butter?'

'Yes, of course. Bellinda, please pass Muzi the butter.'

'Busisiwe, could you please run outside and ask Muzi to be careful with his shears. Those roses are somewhat of a family heirloom. He seems to have forgotten.'

'Do you girls want me or Abriana to read to you tonight?'

This went on until Bell and Busi stopped putting their pyjamas and toothbrushes in their backpacks every morning. Busi had even stopped hiding biscuits in her only clean pair of socks.

Port Elizabeth became home and home-school became a way

of life. Soon they were reading and writing in Siswati, Dutch, Italian, English, Sesotho and French – Bell was the better speaker while Busi mastered the reading and writing of the languages. Muzi did most of the teaching in the afternoons because Abriana was always busy up in her workshop – a large shed in the back-yard. Having been intruders for most of their lives, the girls knew instinctively which places adults didn't want them to enter. Abriana's shed was one of those 'no-go' places.

Childhood curiosity, however, is stronger than the survival instinct of even the most seasoned intruders. It was this curiosity that one day lead Bell to wake up during nap time and drag her sister out of bed. Busi already knew where she was being led to; their language was one without words or explanations – it was instinct and experience. Experience told Busi that Bell had been planning the little adventure since they first moved in and instinct told her that they would end up in trouble. She shook her head but still followed the barefoot intruder. Bell knew that Muzi was not in the house – he did grocery shopping on Wednesdays during nap time. They ran quickly across the backyard to the workshop, where a screeching noise filled the pauses of suburban life. They weren't tall enough to see through the window and Busi refused to let Bell stand on her shoulders. 'No! This is my new, favourite jersey, Bell. No. It has balloons on it, look.' They argued in hushed tones which turned into shoving. With all the frustrated and angry shoulder slamming going on, they didn't notice that the screeching had stopped and Abriana was standing at the door, watching them. 'What are you doing out here?' Her husky voice had never sounded threatening until that moment. She walked towards them and put a hand on each one's shoulder. 'You want to see what I'm doing in there?' Silence was always their best defence so the sisters retreated within, expecting the worst. 'It's okay, I'm not angry. I'm surprised it took you this long to venture here.' Still they kept their silence. Bell, who was always the main instigator, was also the first to burst into tears. Busi widened her eyes at Bell, a silent promise to keep her safe. They both gasped when they walked in and saw the collection of knives on the table. Bell let out a shocked cry that made Abriana realise her mistake.

It took Muzi an hour to calm the girls down; his anger banished Abriana to her workshop. 'Seriously? We agreed that we were going to handle this together.' He was standing outside the kitchen door glaring at his wife while occasionally casting a watchful eye on the children inside.

'I was sharpening the knives. It was an accident.'

'They thought you were going to kill them ... Oh for fuck's sake.'

'Language!' Abriana muttered. The couple sighed and stared at each other.

When Mam' Gladys had called them about two children who were in desperate need of a home, they'd both tried to get out of it.

'You know what we do for a living. What kind of a home would it be? This seems irresponsible ...' But they couldn't say no.

Mam' Gladys had looked after Muzi when he was an orphan; he'd needed more attention, assurance and guidance than the other children at the orphanage. His vitiligo made him difficult to accept; even the most kind-hearted couples didn't want a child people would stare at. There was already so much hateful pseudo-science and division based on skin. After a second family brought him back to the orphanage, Mam' Gladys called a friend. She had grown tired of exposing children to the monstrosities of adults; every few years she encountered children who had seen too much ugliness and would never know anything else. These children, who had become accustomed to the hatred that hides behind civility, she would entrust only to people who hunted monsters. She knew that these children had, from pure survival, developed an internal homing device for the unbelievable and frightening things that existed. 'Help them use their unwanted gift,' is what Mam' Gladys asked of Abriana and Muzi for Bellinda and Busi.

'Should we just go to Cape Town?'

'No, Bell. We are in Bloem for a reason: the Vera.'

'So we are just going to ignore the Cape Town situation?'

'Werewolves ...' Busi flinched as she said the word; there was a family sitting nearby. She was always careful not to say something that would make people suspicious of them. When they were teenagers, people assumed that they were criminals, runaways, sex workers or (even worse) strangers who were looking for trouble. There was also the danger of human predators hunting them while they hunted monsters. Bell always told Busi that there was very little difference between the two: 'They'll both kill you, human or ghoul.'

The car had started making spluttering sounds so she pulled up at a pit-stop garage, one of those stops where families on road trips across the country took breaks to stretch their legs, get snacks and let their kids be someone else's problem for a while.

Lowering her voice, Busi continued: 'Werewolves are a pack and packs don't just move. It isn't even full moon.' Bell let out a forced laugh. 'The pack we are after defies that full moon sh … stuff. You know that.'

'Mam' Gladys said the Vera is getting violent, Bell.'

'Aaargh, do we have to do everything The Immortal tells us to do?'

Busi spat out her Coke and rum, laughing until the family nearby gave the sisters a dirty look. Bell was convinced Mam' Gladys was immortal, much to Busi's amusement. It was easier to be amused than accept that perhaps there was some truth to what her sister believed. Why did Mam' Gladys hardly seem to age? Black doesn't crack, but surely it still tires? Nobody knew how old she was and her biggest anti-ageing secret was 'drink water and don't live with men'.

Bell was rolling her eyes but the man was genuinely terrified. She sighed and tied her hair up while he told his story.

'The ghost fondled you?' she asked, with a hairpin lodged between her teeth.

The man folded the edges of the flyers for a micro-money-lender that he was supposed to be handing out. He turned to Busi who was holding a phone close to his face to record his story. 'Eish, sester, can you switch that thing off please?' Busi put the phone in her backpack, handed Bell the flyers and gently guided the man into the tiny café behind them. It smelled of old oil and yeast. Sometimes the information-gathering process needed a little bit of patience. Bell was impossibly impatient and she couldn't stand it when people stared at her scar while she spoke. Busi really didn't like dealing with people either but considered it an occupational hazard. She once called it that in front of Mam' Gladys and, from the corner of her eye, saw the (not so) old woman's face slowly turn into a picture of sadness. Busi often got the feeling that Mam' Gladys wished they had grown up like other children, where the only monsters were human.

'Bheki,' she used his name to put him at ease, 'tell me what happened.' He accepted the bottle of Coke she handed him and swallowed hard before opening up both bottle and himself.

It was a Thursday night that felt like a Friday because December is made up of Fridays only. Bheki was in the last taxi home ('transport here is a joke, sester') when the driver told him he needed to fill up at a nearby petrol station. There was nobody else in the vehicle and the driver offered to drop him off right outside his gate, so Bheki didn't complain. Alcohol was forcing his eyes closed but the ears remained open; he heard the driver talking to someone – presumably the petrol attendant. The door behind him opened and he heard the driver joke about 'drunk women throwing away their dignity in December', and more jokes that only men found funny. The driver's door opened and closed and they were on their way again. Bheki heard a sharp gasp ('the driver ... he didn't look right, sester') that made him open his eyes. 'It was a woman's name that he said.'

Busi already knew the rest of the story. The driver crashed into a pole and died on impact. It was the shock of seeing his (dead) ex-girlfriend in the rear-view mirror that made him lose control of the wheel. Bheki didn't know that then – his concern was for the other passenger and alcohol had numbed his survival instincts. He turned around to see if the person behind him was okay. It was a woman ('she looked young, sester, but she wasn't afraid or shocked'). The next thing, the young woman was no longer in the back seat but sitting right beside him, smiling and touching him while the driver bled to death in front of her. 'Something didn't feel right, sester.' When she leaned in to say something, he opened the door and ran to the police station. 'I didn't want to hear what she was saying.' He was growing angrier as he spoke; fear did that to men. Busi stroked the knife in her jacket pocket; angry men made her nervous. She focused her eyes on Bell who was pressing flyers into people's hands, even those who shook their heads politely.

'The guys at the petrol station said nobody else got into the taxi. But I saw her. Do you hear me? I saw the woman! She touched me …' Busi lifted the bottle of Coke up to Bheki's face. He took a sip and a few deep breaths.

The Woman Who Wasn't There drove Bheki halfway between madness and desperation, so he started his own investigation. It did nothing to soothe him because the name he heard uttered that night was that of the taxi driver's ex-girlfriend. Friends and family of the driver were reluctant to talk to the only person who'd survived the crash. Grief does that; it makes people want to find someone to blame for the death of a loved one. Nonetheless, Bheki persisted until, somehow, a story of abuse emerged: Taxi Driver meets Young Woman, she works nights, he's constantly on the road, he picks her up from work one night, they get into a fight, he loses his temper and leaves her on the side of the road, the night swallows her up and spits out her dead body in a field weeks later.

'Am I crazy, my sister?' Busi shook her head and got up. Standing at the door of the small café she made eye contact with

Bell who sighed. They both hated hunting Veras because they were always violent. Not as violent as Werewolves though – there was nothing they hated more than Werewolves. She could feel Bheki staring at her; she turned around so he could ask the question that men haunted by Veras always ask. Bheki looked at his shoes and took a long sip of Coke.

'We would never have to deal with a Vera if men would stop killing women,' Bell said, leaning closer. Busi pushed her back and listened to Mam' Gladys through the speaker phone: 'Please carry on, Mama.' Mam' Gladys was listing all the deaths of women in Bloemfontein before the Vera appeared, and the death of men following its appearance. 'This Vera won't stop killing. You know what to do. Nibe be careful please.' With that Mam' Gladys hung up.

After an hour of trying to gather more information, Bell placed the laptop gently on her sister's lap. It had been a while since the letters jumped around like this, confusing her. Busi knew it was heartbreak that was making the words play musical chairs with her sister. Moving around as parentless and virtually homeless monster-hunting teenagers was difficult for Bell: too many tearful goodbyes and vials filled with perfume from the ones she fell in love with (she called them Lover's Tears). It was Vial 20 that did it this time. Vial 20: a short girl with blonde dreadlocks; she was always trailed by the smell of chamomile. Busi preferred to remember them by their Vial numbers because names were useless to her; they would only have to be replaced by new ones anyway. Romance didn't make sense to her, neither did attraction. It was something she was happy to be privy to as a witness to her sister's life but never as an active member. People were messy and mean.

Bell was complaining about hunger when there was a knock at the door. Mam' Gladys had a network of friends who housed them when they hunted. If there was no friend with a back room or spare bedroom, they stayed at ancient hotels above old bars. Every town had a neglected 'heritage' building that smelled like damp carpets. Towns forgotten by time always seemed to be haunted by or were home to some lonely, ancient monster. 'There are no curses. This is a country built by the labour of many abused people, whose progeny was also further abused. Small towns are full of vengeful spirits,' Muzi once said to Bell, when she suggested that small towns were cursed. In Bloemfontein, they had a friend with a back room that was comfortable enough for two people who were used to sleeping on floors and never really attached to the comforts of having 'your own things'.

The knock was a food delivery by a small, pale boy who was both frightened and thrilled by the handle of a dagger peaking from the back of Bell's jeans. He closed the door reluctantly after Bell gave him a fist bump.

'I think I know what's happening here,' Busi said, while eyeing the tripe and pap on the plate. Bell was already getting stuck in, licking at the gravy that was running down her forearm. Mother Four took them back to the children's home precisely because Bell insisted on acting like a feral child. She wouldn't use utensils and once ate a scab while looking Mother Four in the eye. Family Six rejecting them was Busi's fault. Everybody knew Bell couldn't read under pressure; the letters tricked her and she had to concentrate extra hard just to make them behave. Father Six was an impatient type who was unfamiliar with kindness; he called Bell a moron while helping her with her homework. Busi intended to carve MORON on his face but the knife only managed to make a broken M before Mother Six pulled her off and locked her in a wardrobe for an entire night.

Hunting Veras was always violent. Always. The second one they ever hunted gave Bell the scar that made her seem like she was perpetually smiling, a slice down the right side of her mouth – compliments of the furious Vera. They are called Veras because many years ago, residents of a township were haunted by a ghost named Vera. At least, that was the face the thing took on. The stories all differ because a Vera is a collection of energies emboldened by a particularly cruel death. Mam' Gladys told them that death had stopped being sad or shocking, particularly the death of women at the hands of men. The sadness, pain and fear of the women left behind in the violence calls on the dead women as protectors or avengers. For whatever reason, Veras love tormenting men in vehicles. A train driver nods off and wakes up to see his deceased childhood sweetheart standing in front of the locomotive. That train driver's love killed herself after he rejected her. The last Vera Busi and Bell hunted was emboldened by the suicide of a teenage girl who was bullied terribly after a stupid boy she trusted shared naked photos of her. It was a small town, much like the one they were in. What is it with small towns?

'Remember when Mama and Baba took us on a Vera hunt?' Busi asked, after explaining what they were up against. 'Well, we hid in the trailer; they didn't exactly take us ... Was that in Soweto?'

'Yeah. And you kept complaining about the smell.'

'These things are gross, man. I swear ... Remember when I threw up after my first poltergeist?'

'The one that punched you in your teenage boob?'

'Dude! I swear that breast is smaller than the right one. Fucking ghost.'

Busi stopped laughing and looked at her left hand. Her hand would always be a reminder of the night they lost the only family they knew to ambush by a pack of Werewolves; it wasn't even full moon.

Bell grew silent too. 'I promise we will find them, B.'

'For what?'

'Revenge.' Busi started packing her backpack. 'We have a Vera to put to bed.'

'Sounds like one of my nights out.'

Bell's joke fell between them and rolled under the bed. She fished something out of her bag and pushed it under her sister's nose. 'Go on. You know you want it.'

Busi grabbed the box and tore the wrapping open. They held each other as Busi's chest heaved violently with sobs.

'Shhhh. I would never forget. Happy birthday, m'takama. You're the best little sister in the world.'

Busi looked down at her wrist, admiring her gift, a silver

bracelet. Small letters hung between the loops: M. O. R. O. N.

Bell stroked the place where the pinkie and ring finger were missing on her sister's hand. 'I'm going to kill those filthy animals. Full moon or not.'

Busi smiled and wiped her nose.

'Can we do this already?' She threw the keys to their pale-blue Ford Cortina to Bell. 'I wanna get out of Bloemfontein ... like yesterday!'

On the Run

by Mokwadi Fela*

[Disclosure: Some names have been changed and locations have not been named.]

The people I interview are used to the attention that comes with their jobs. Rappers, movie stars, soapie actors, *Top Billing* presenters, rugby players, football stars and their model wives, etc. There is always a hint of arse kissing and the occasional side eye when I ask questions that could embarrass the star. There are also unfortunate incidents like when a certain journalist was left stranded at East London airport after a studio interview (with the Rapper Who Tried To Sue Her) turned into a plane ride to another province because 'everybody wants a piece of me and the sky is the only place they can't reach me'. I'm in the business of profiling and indulging famous people.

Nolwazi Botha didn't ask for fame but she is certainly one of the most recognisable women in the world. You know you're famous when your face is spray-painted all over downtown Johannesburg. The cool kids wear T-shirts with her face and nickname plastered across the front. Gqom and other hip-hop artists name-check her in their songs and she is fondly known as Sister Alterado by her fans and supporters. It's difficult to believe that a woman who was accused of murder (she escaped before her trial began) and is now a fugitive has fans, but she does.

A year ago, many South Africans had never heard of The Alterado (Portuguese for 'altered'). They are the group who turned Nolwazi Botha into the Most Wanted Woman in South Africa. On a cold winter's morning, prisoners at Johannesburg Correctional Centre (also known as Sun City Prison) reported hearing a loud bang – it came from the women's section of the prison. It would take the Department of Correctional Services two entire days to hold a press conference explaining that Nolwazi Botha had escaped from jail. Through investigative journalism that would make Debora Patta proud, details slowly emerged that an entire wall of the prison had been blown up and that it was the work of a Terrorist Group called The Alterado.

The Alterado sounds like the name of a band that would be on the Afropunk line-up. Interpol's Counter Terrorism Programme doesn't have much information on them (they should enlist the help of the people who were so keen to Find Kony – they had more information than Interpol). There are a few articles online where they are briefly mentioned as being responsible for the 'kidnapping' of prisoners in Rwanda, Uganda, Egypt and even Eritrea. Nolwazi Botha thrust them into international notoriety.

When I was a Baby Journalist, I dreamed of an assignment like this; the reality was frightening and unbelievable. Sean Penn had El Chapo; I have Nolwazi Botha aka Sister Alterado.

This all began, a few months ago, with a seemingly harmless message on WhatsApp – from an unknown number. It went unread for a few days (who answers messages from unknown numbers?). During a very trying interview with an actor (who shall remain unnamed), I received a series of photos from the unknown number and a text simply saying, 'Check WhatsApp. Much more interesting than boring thespian.' I assumed it was one of my friends being funny (or weird). As it turned out, my interview with the thespian was cut short because he could never be as interesting as the photos I received: South Africa's most wanted woman holding up pieces of paper with the words 'I want to talk to you'. I wish I could tell you how they found me but they didn't tell me (believe me, I asked).

Let me be completely honest: A lot of what was done to get this interview was both stupid and daring … mostly stupid because I was in contact with The Alterado and eventually allowed them to take me, and a photographer, to an undisclosed location – meaning I can't include information about how we got there (train, bus, etc.), who picked us up and where we went. I'm learning from Sean Penn's mistakes.

This is the part of the interview where I describe what the star/personality is wearing. Nolwazi Botha is a normal-looking woman; she is not the dangerous creature that most people would expect. Her thick black dreadlocks grow past her shoulders and occasionally she twirls a few around her index finger when she gets nervous or worked up. Twitter users have turned this ordinary-looking woman into a meme (standard practice) and a verb. 'I will Botha the next man who asks me to smile, strusgod,' tweets Twitter user @notyourissaray. 'To Botha' is now a colloquial term for killing a man. Much like the way to 'Tsafenda' is used to mean stabbing someone – after Dimitri Tsafendas who assassinated Prime Minister Hendrik Verwoerd in 1966.

Botha flinches when I mention Domestic Androcide. Men's

Rights Activists have taken to their keyboards and made her the face of what many Feminists are calling a fallacy and false equivalence.

NB: Domestic Andro ... No, please. Those people are saying that I'm the new Lorena Bobbitt. Can you imagine? This is not what it looks like. I'm not a monster.

MF: Isn't she the woman who chopped her husband's penis off?

NB: Yes. They must have had problems. Eugene and I didn't have problems. He was never cruel to me. We grew up together ... neighbours. He was my best friend. It was hard, you know.

MF: You mean being adopted?

NB: Yeah. It was in the early 90s and I didn't know why people had such strong reactions to my presence. My parents also didn't know what to do. They did their best.

MF: Let's go back to the beginning, because your adoption story is unconventional.

NB: (chuckles) Oh gosh. My dad told this story a lot when I was a teenager. It was a safer time and my adoption was official by then. Daddy Sherman would have a few drinks before he started telling this story. He would always call me his Durban Poison

Baby ... Like the marijuana ... Anyway. Dad was a young, dumb, white liberal on a road trip to KZN with my Uncle Pete. This was in the 1990s – a different time. They picked up some hitchhikers and went along the coast picking up and dropping off various people. One of those people was a young man called Bambatha. He basically told Daddy and Uncle Pete that he was an ANC member who was making his way home to KwaDukuza ... some people still call it Stanger. Anyway, he promised Daddy and Uncle Pete proper strong weed, not the majat they were smoking. They dropped him off outside his house and he said he would have the stuff when they came back from their road trip.

MF: Wait ... Two white boys just driving in and out of what were then black areas?

NB: Yep. Daddy is still like that. He figures fear is what makes places dangerous.

MF: What?!

NB: (laughing) I know. He's the best. Anyway they went on their merry way and on their way back were looking forward to the promised weed. Of course this was the 90s and political violence was hectic. IFP and ANC people got into it over whatever. You know how it was back then. The street leading to Bambatha's home was blocked. Daddy and Uncle Pete were still determined to get that Durban Poison for their trip back to Johannesburg. They basically talked their way out of the scrimmage by assuring the people with red bandanas that they weren't cops, just some dumb white kids. They finally make it to Bambatha's house and find his mother, who is scared for her life because 'more white men looking for my son'. She was convinced they were like proper cops. Special Branch even! She tells them to stay indoors while she goes to his secret hiding place. Comes back a few minutes later and tells them he's gone back to the bush – code for he's probably on his way out of the country via ANC secret pathways. They're bummed because there is no weed for the trip back home but they get back into their VW Kombi and head out. About three hours later, Uncle Pete and Daddy get the scare of their frikkin lives. A little girl starts crying in the back of their Kombi. Uncle Pete thought it was a tokoloshe. (uncontrollable laughter)

MF: But it was you.

NB: Yep, with a note attached to my vest. Saying, 'This is Nolwazi, she is three.' My date of birth and a line saying, 'The bad people. They will be coming for her. Please leave with a good black family. God bless you.' That was it. Uncle Pete was freaked out because he was still living with his parents after he served in

97

the military. He knew they would not accept me. Daddy was already married and he came up with the idea of pretending I was the domestic worker's child until she could help them find me a home. What a bunch of liberals.

Our conversation is paused when Nolwazi asks for a cigarette break. She informs me that it's a habit she picked up in prison. The view from the stoep of the cabin is breathtaking and that's all I am allowed to say about that. (Botha was given a copy of this interview before we went to print. She removed any identifying descriptions of where we were, for her and everyone's safety.) It's a warm winter's day, so we decide to have tea out on the stoep. There were some members of The Alterado situated all around the yard of the house we were in. We could have been a large family holidaying in the bush. Except maybe for the four guys with guns, everybody else seemed really relaxed and they would occasionally look up at us or check if we needed something.

MF: You met Eugene when you were kids?

NB: Yes. He lived next door and his father was a widower. I never felt 'othered' by him. He would always come over and speak to me in Afrikaans ... very patiently, until I knew a few words. I still spoke a little bit of isiZulu so he learned a few words of that too. Daddy brought me home and Moran took one look at me and decided I was their child. Mom has a way of making things go her way. Always! She was fond of Eugene because he didn't have a mom, so we grew up in the same house, pretty much.

MF: Was it weird when you started dating?

NB: No. It was the night of his matric dance and he came over to show Mom his tuxedo. Oom Jan, his dad, was used to sharing him with us so he walked him over. I was sulking in my pyjamas because it felt like Eugene was growing away from me. We took a few photos ... I wonder where those photos are now? Probably with Oom ... He hates me. I never got to explain. So much guilt while I was in prison. But this is all his fault. He knows it is.

MF: What happened the night of the matric dance?

NB: Oh. Sorry. I went to my room after photos and assumed that Eugene had left. A few minutes later there was a knock at my door. Eugene came in, lay in bed next to me and said he was sorry that he didn't ask me to the matric dance. I don't know whether he meant it but it made me feel better. He kissed me. Like full on Frenching. (giggles) It was nice. I guess that was the beginning of our thing. It always felt right with him. We got married as soon as we both got our degrees. It seems like everything was so simple.

MF: Until that night in June?

NB: (nods)

MF: What happened that night?

NB: You're smart. You read the transcripts from court and what the police say happened.

MF: Yes. But I want to hear it in your own words.

Nolwazi wraps her arms around herself and looks at the teacup next to her. She's reluctant to talk and I allow the hurt to sit between us until she is ready.

NB: I had come home late. It was date night and Eugene was already showered and ready for supper. My phone had died so he must have been frustrated or tired of trying to call me. He hated being angry and that made him even angrier. He lost his English when he was angry. It was just Afrikaans one way and sometimes I wasn't sure exactly what he was saying. That night he was tired, I was tired and it was just stupid couple stuff. We were trying to have a baby; IVF wasn't taking. I wanted to give up. He wanted to keep trying. We were tired but it was nothing major. Not like how your colleagues at the newspapers made it seem. (glares at me)

MF: I'm sorry about that. Part of the job, I guess.

NB: Your job sucks.

We sit in silence for five minutes.

NB: He just wanted to keep arguing and I kept asking him for space. We were standing in the passage and I opened the bathroom door to get away from him. He wasn't yelling but he was antagonising me. I shut the door in his face and everything else is a blur. It was like there was a ringing in my ears, but really loud and sore, you know? Like when you have an inner ear infection. I couldn't see properly and it looked like the veins in my arms were bulging. This won't make sense but it felt like there was fire in my veins. That fire was anger. Am I making sense?

MF: Did he open the door?

NB: I think so. I don't know what happened but I knew immediately that I had done something terrible. I was covered in blood. People say that, but I was actually covered in blood and vomit. I threw up when I saw one of Eugene's legs in the passage. I was crawling towards the door. They say I was hysterical but I don't remember that.

MF: The police report said your neighbours heard you

screaming ... for what sounded like a long time.

NB: I swear it felt like it all happened in a few minutes. I would never hurt Eugene. I didn't do this ...

When the story first broke, it was just a few lines on the fifth page of a newspaper. A young journalist sitting in court waiting for something juicy made it a bigger story a few weeks later. A police officer on a cigarette break, with verbal diarrhoea, pointed to a prisoner who'd chopped her husband to pieces. The young journalist followed up and broke what would be the most talked-about murder case in (new) South Africa. Daily newspapers speculated on possible motives: money, a new lover, race, abuse, and they spoke to all possible 'experts'. One of them, a most nauseating human and men's rights activist, was given half a page to explore the Domestic Androcide angle. Jan Botha, Nolwazi's estranged father-in-law, was very quick to condemn and vilify his daughter-in-law. On camera he appeared to be a man suppressing a lot of anger – rightfully so, after having lost his son in such a brutal way. A clip that CNN played over and over was of him outside the court in a suit that looked like it had once fit, but not anymore; grief and shock had shrunk him. He was choking back tears – 'how can a person carry on living knowing their only child was ripped ... or chopped ... to pieces? How am I supposed to live now?'

MF: How are your parents?

NB: I don't know but I have great guilt about hurting the people who took me in and raised me. You know they were staying with friends, during the trial. They were getting hate calls and being threatened. I can't imagine how they are now. They must be so confused. Thank God they sold that house where I grew up. I can't imagine them having to see that awful man every day ... (sigh)

MF: Why do you call Jan 'that awful man'?

NB: That's why you're here, right? You want to know why a deranged, violent woman would hate her father-in-law? Well ... My birth father, Bambatha, was an MK operative. He was used to going in and out of the country but one time he got caught and it wasn't by the plain old stupid dangerous police. It was by evil itself. The kind of Special Branch police that captured, tortured and turned people into Askaris or whatever ... Some of the prisoners they couldn't turn were handed over to a few doctors who specialised in experimenting on humans for God knows what. There were many of these types of ambitious, hateful doctors who were serving their countries and going against the Hippocratic Oath. You know wherever there is war, you find doctors like that. Like that German one: Mengele. My father-in-law was one of those doctors.

MF: You're saying your father-in-law was an apartheid death doctor who experimented on your biological father?

NB: (smirks) I know what it sounds like – it sounds like I'm some unhinged fugitive. But Jan was working on some super soldier project and once he was done with his human lab rats, he made sure they were disposed of. Bambatha and two other captives managed to escape. They were given some kind of sedative by another one of those ambitious killer doctors but it didn't work on them. Bambatha went back home and kept moving in and out of the country. In his hometown my mother gave birth to me. She had become an MK operative too. She was in Angola and I was being raised by Bambatha's mother. I don't know what happened to them. Maybe they're dead, but whatever happened to me was because of Jan Botha.

MF: What are the chances that you would end up living next door to the man who experimented on your father?

NB: This fucking country, man! What makes you so sure that you aren't in line at the post office or supermarket next to one of those apartheid death squad people? In your newsroom or whatever, who's to say that half those people didn't vote for the National Party with pride and would do it again?

MF: Maybe. But none of them ever experimented on my parents.

NB: Well lucky you. I'll be sure to get you a medal before you go.

MF: What I mean is, it's unbelievable. Listen, most people reading this are going to think you're a fugitive who is blaming the father of the man she killed for ...

NB: For ruining my life? Yes. When I was in prison, some people wanted to prove that I'm not a monster. You know ... prove that I was just human and not a saint, like some activists were saying, or a monster like you media people were portraying me. A woman who had killed her son – he was a rapist – was the first to attack me. I grew up in the suburbs and suddenly now I had to be faced with violence every day. This wild son-killer woman was going to beat me till 'every bone in your bitch body is broken'. Those were her exact words. I didn't know this woman but she was so angry with me.

MF: Did you ever find out why? Why she was angry with you?

N.B: After I broke both her arms, one of her little minions

told me that I was taking up too much media attention. Seems our country only has appetite for one sad woman story at a time.

M.F: Wait, go back a bit. You broke her arms?

N.B: Yes. It turns out that the fire in my veins makes me some kind of scary, angry, super-strong person. That fire is usually fear but anger works just as well. A doctor in Mozambique did a brain scan, and basically he said that something has changed the size and shape of my hypothalamus. So I am essentially broken forever and I know it's because of Jan. There are others like me who were either experimented on or are the children of those people. That's why Alterado. It means we are altered forever by the actions of hateful people. I don't know how they knew that I was one of them, but they showed up that morning and broke me out of jail. I was in a bad way – really afraid that I was either going to kill someone or be killed.

MF: Is he one of them? (pointing at the baby sleeping on the sofa next to her)

NB: Ha ha ha. That's my son. We'd stopped taking pregnancy tests; there was no way to know that I was already pregnant. Some of our doctors reckon that falling pregnant had something to do with my powers kicking in.

MF: What kind of things set you off?

NB: Interesting choice of words, 'set me off'. I guess I am kind of like a bomb in many ways. When they first rescued me, I was in solitary for hurting too many people. I knew that I needed to learn how to control it, so they threw me in the deep end. A few of my new brothers and sisters have ugly scars because of me. Luckily there was only one with broken bones – and it was a girl who can heal herself quickly. Like magic! She's one of the people who brought you here.

MF: What do you mean by 'deep end'?

NB: Well … we are like a family. And it's your family that trains or prepares you for the outside world. Let's just say they pushed my fear and anger to the limit, to see what I'm capable of. Sounds extreme, I know.

MF: What's the plan, Nolwazi?

NB: Honestly …? I can't go home, and I want to keep my baby safe. I also want the nightmares to stop.

MF: Nightmares?

NB: Yes. I keep dreaming that Jan is coming for us because he considers us his property. In the dreams Eugene is alive but Jan has made him half machine, half robot and they are hell-bent on taking my baby away.

MF: Are you ever going to be at peace?

NB: Maybe after you publish the documents that we acquired … Jan wanted to keep them hidden forever. He's not the only one. There are many people in power who are implicated and they are going to have to answer for their part in hurting so many people. Hopefully the truth will give me peace … Somehow I doubt it.

Our interview ended when Botha's son, whose name she refused to share, woke up and she got up slowly to soothe him. Tucked under the cushion where her son was sleeping, was an envelope that she pulled out and handed to me. 'Make sure the world knows what happened to us and our parents.' I clutched the envelope and wondered if I would ever see this strangely gentle woman, who calls a terrorist organisation her family, again. I was escorted back to a location I cannot disclose. I sat next to a young woman who had the smoothest skin I'd ever seen. I asked her if she was the self-healing one and she just laughed. On the way, I read the files Botha handed me and knew immediately that I would never see her again, because as crazy as she sounded, it seemed she had receipts (as the kids say): photos, official documents, eye-witness accounts, bank statements of certain high-profile businessmen and politicians (pre- and post-1994) and doctor's charts.

Next week, we expose the men behind some of the biggest human right's violations in South Africa, Swaziland and Mozambique.

* To protect the identity of the writer/s who worked on this story, we have decided to give them an alias. Mokwadi Fela literally means 'just a writer'.

Little Vultures

'There's death somewhere on my land.' My voice sounded like it was far away.

'Nokuzola, why do you have to talk like that? Are you a cowboy sheriff? Anyway … I'm ready for a new face. New decade, new face. Who wants to look the same forever?' Ingrid put her glass of whiskey down and grabbed the skin around her jaw. 'This has to go, obviously.'

I looked away from her and back to the window in front of me. There were too many butterflies. That could only mean death. 'Can we go see if my animals are okay?'

Ingrid sighed, reached for her cane and pulled herself up. 'Is this about the butterflies?'

I nodded and put my work boots on. 'They are tiny little vultures.'

When Frank died, his children expected me to move back to the city and allow them to take ownership of our farm. Vile children! They never liked me and hardly ever checked on their father when he was alive. Yes, I was a young woman who married a wealthy older man but it was never about money. Frank was kind, sensual and genuinely supportive of my work, and he understood why I could never go back to the city. It wasn't the death threats, although there was a time when they kept me up at night. There was no coming back from the fall-out of Baby A and people weren't ready to forget. So I ran away to the less loved parts of the country. The parts where we could develop our own piece of heaven that would eventually include animals that were free to roam within the boundaries of the sonic gates – who knows what people would do if they sighted a quagga running alongside a mini mammoth? Probably close the death circle that I had opened. My poor dodos wouldn't last a week out there. And what of Donto, or Dino Dog as Ingrid calls him? The world is not ready to know that there is an unusually large (for its species) Heterodontosaurus running around out of its own time.

Before the animals, it was the babies. My research turned Baby A into a reality. Two females made a baby and it was an abomination according to those who were spokespeople for the gods. Men who worshipped Science questioned my methods but really they were questioning their own failures. Many in my field balked at my research, but it was really about pedigree: not only was I my family's first genomicist but I was also our first graduate. My colleagues and I didn't know we could do it, but we tried. We failed until we succeeded and didn't sleep properly for seven months. Baby A turned out perfect. Too perfect, because my mentor and supervisor stole some of my research and soon became the face of 'We will do it ethically next time. My ambitious apprentice kept pushing even when I advised against it.' He went on to sell designer babies for those who've always wondered what a Naomi Campbell and Kendall Jenner baby would look like. He used the names of vintage models to dampen the horror of what he was actually proposing. They all failed; none of the babies made it to term but the damage was done.

We named him Baby A after the first man in creation. Hubris, I know. I often wonder how he is and if his mothers will ever tell him the true story of his birth.

The city was driving me to unbearable headaches – I couldn't hear myself anymore. It was like my inside voice was being drowned out by the hate. When Frank first suggested that we move, I was horrified – I was born in the city and always thought I would die in one. 'We can create our own little heaven. You can have your own lab. I'll read all the books I've been meaning to read.' We fantasised about idyllic days until we were hungry for it to become a reality.

With Frank, I was happy and at peace until he died. He fell one morning while making his way from the house to the lab. At a certain age, a fall is not a laughing matter that you can just dust off. Frank was at that age. When it was clear that the children weren't getting anything, they fought me. Dragged me in and out of courts until they couldn't afford it anymore. Even after that they showed up on my property with fake humility asking that I help pay their legal fees. I set Bron (a fantastic lab mistake that became a horse-sized dodo) onto them and they left a cloud of dust behind them. Bloody cowards. The house was lonely without Frank but my animals kept me company; I spent most of my time camping by the river.

The butterflies announced Ingrid's arrival. It was early morning when I noticed more than one of those beautiful monsters congregating together. They aren't social so I knew something was off. My first thought was that one of my animals had fallen ill or died so I got into my van and drove to the river, their favourite place on the property.

It was on my way back to the house that I discovered Ingrid outside the gate — no shoes, bloody soles, bleeding from the head, both hands clutching the massive gate. Her car was a few metres away, also battered. She was a bloody body covered with those colourful scavengers. I wished I had bothered to learn their language because I could have reached Ingrid faster.

As I watched her sleeping in the guest bedroom downstairs, it was clear that she would never leave. The outside world was foreign to me but her face wasn't. I would have had to be in a cave not to know that she performed on stages all over the world. A remarkable pianist with a strange desire to alter her face continually. *I'm not obsessed with youth; I'm just obsessed with looking good.* She was thinking that when she finally came to and asked for a mirror. I must have looked shocked because her inside voice was loud and angry. 'I'm not judging you,' I said as I took the mirror away from her. 'Did I say you were?' She looked confused because no words had been exchanged between us. 'And anyway, I don't really care what people think of me.' I could tell she meant that too, because there was no internal follow-up. Ingrid never told me why she had been driving under the influence of too many shots of whiskey and painkillers for no pain but I told her she could stay for as long as she wanted. She shrugged and said, 'I bet my fans are wondering what happened to me.' It was followed by a small internal *thank you*.

Some days I don't see her at all – the benefit of having a large house and spending most of my days by the river with my pets or in the lab. One day she walked into the kitchen with her face covered in bandages. I gasped and she shook her head at me. *Don't you dare make me laugh, you bitch*, was what her inside voice said. I collapsed into a giggling fit. 'You didn't even notice that I was gone,' she chided, with what she meant to be mock shock. I had been camping out in the field and had no idea she'd even left the house.

'You won't be able to breathe soon, wena. Where is the rest of your nose?' Ingrid waved away my comment and made herself a smoothie consisting of celery, cod liver oil, spinach, water and a green powder that made her cough when she scooped it into the blender. The smoothies were part of her Stay Supple Forever mission – that and the daily yoga outside Violet's rondawel.

'She's up to something, you know.' Ingrid was very suspicious of Violet, ever since the day she came over for brunch and didn't leave. Ingrid's lips didn't move but she knew I could hear her as she walked out. *You shouldn't have shown her your work.*

My ability to hear what people were thinking came to me when I was a young girl. Mme used to laugh a lot, a big, breast-shaking, uvula-revealing laugh. I can count on my hand the number of times I saw her frown or cry. The first was when her best friend and second mother to me, Aus' Gertrude, died. They were inseparable. We would get off the train and walk to Aus' Gertrude's house during the week. Aus' Gertrude would help me with my homework while Mme cooked supper for us. Most people felt sorry for them – two unwed women, spending all their time together. But I was in on the secret, albeit accidentally. Aus' Gertrude and Mme loved each other in the way my friends' parents did. Sometimes, while Aus' Gertrude was helping me with maths problems, she would look up at Mme and think, *This is perfect ... Goodness, you're beautiful ... The love of my life.* I could hear it but Mme couldn't.

Aus' Gertrude died in a car accident on her way back from Qwaqwa, where she had been working for a few months. Mme cried when she heard; she cried when her boss refused to give her time off to attend the funeral in Qwaqwa, and when I told her how much Aus' Gertrude loved her. She cried again when I told her that I could hear what people were thinking. Not surprised, just fearful, she looked at me, wiped her eyes and said: 'There aren't many people like you, Nokuzola. Find them, hold them close, and protect each other.' Mme also impressed on me that I had to learn to 'mind my own business' because listening in on people's thoughts was intrusive, and everyone was entitled to their secrets. So I learned to turn the thoughts into static that could become words when I wanted to intrude.

I guess you could say my work is conservation – conservation of extinct animals. That's what made Violet stay. Ingrid took one look at her and thought, *oh, no. Not another sad, wounded type. Didn't we just heal that sick quagga last week?* I giggled because all she did was shout orders from a safe distance while the quagga gave birth. It was our first live birth and Ingrid remembered it as 'a sick quagga'.

Violet must have called again and again until I had no choice but to answer the home phone. She sounded sad and desperate, so I invited her to brunch. She ate like a woman who had not seen or smelled food in weeks, much to Ingrid's chagrin. I couldn't understand many of her thoughts because they were so jumbled up, but there was definitely something there about loss and anger. When we were at university, Violet was one of the most clear-minded people I knew, her thoughts always orderly and concise. Out of all the people in our genetics class, she was the brightest. The woman who all but inhaled the plates at brunch now was just a shadow – no discernible features or coherent inside voice.

Ingrid cornered me in the kitchen. 'That woman is unhinged. You can't take in strays all the time. This is not a hospital for broken things.'

'Ingrid … I literally found you hanging onto my gate and now you live here.'

'Yes, but I'm helping you while I take a break from fame. I don't suppose geneticists like her have adoring fans waiting for the comeback tour.'

'She can stay as long as she needs to.'

Violet's rondawel was one of four behind the house. It was Frank's idea to have a guesthouse for people who needed to get away from the city. The rondawels were far enough away for the occupants' thoughts not to infiltrate my space. The guesthouse idea never happened because Frank died and I didn't want to see any people on my property. Violet preferred not to be in the house with Ingrid and me.

'She's up to something out there, I'm telling you, Nokuzola.'
Ingrid was annoyed that we had gone 'all the way out there' only
to find nothing related to the little vulture butterflies. I suggested
that since we were driving around, we should go visit Violet and
check up on her.

'Well then you can bust her doing something awful,' I said as
I helped Ingrid out of the SUV. She poked me with her walking
stick and stuck her tongue out at me. The car accident had left
her with a permanent limp and her cane had become an ever-
ready weapon.

Violet only answered the door after five minutes of Ingrid
screaming her name. 'Vaaaaai-let! Vaaaaaai-let. Let us iiiiiiiiiin.
My foot is killing me. Vaaaaaaaaai-let! You know there was
almost a riot in Nairobi when my opening act went five minutes
over time. Now I know how they felt. Vaaaaai-let!'

I was ready to knock the door down myself by the time she
opened it.

'I wasn't expecting company,' Violet said, leading us to her sitting room. She had painted most of the rooms white. I didn't like
it. Frank had all the rondawels painted with Ndebele patterns and
inside each room was a different colour. The one Violet occupied
had been painted different shades of blue.

'We haven't seen you in a while. What have you been up to?'
I asked. But what I really wanted to ask was why she had erased
Frank from the walls. Violet was always difficult to read but I
could hear her now, trying not to get read: *Ask about tea ... Not
butterflies ... Why is she putting her lame leg on my sofa? Can she not
see it's white? ... Not the ... Ask about the animals... Not the ... They
are really visiting? Not the lab. Don't say anyth—* She frowned and
glared at me, knowing that her secret was no longer something
that belonged only to her. 'Zola, I told you many years ago to
stay out of my mind!'

The outburst was unexpected only to someone who was not
privy to Violet's mental gymnastics. Ingrid's eyebrows shot up.
'What did you hear? I knew she was up to something,' she said,
rubbing one knee and holding a cup of Irish coffee in the other
hand. I shrugged and sipped my tea.

This is too much. This bitch is crazy. Even Ingrid knew better than
to say it aloud. She looked over at me to ensure I had heard what
she'd thought.

She was defiant; you could see it in her eyes. Violet was ready for
a fight – I could hear it in her breathing and I saw it in the way
she squeezed her hands into fists. I couldn't take my eyes off what

was behind her. 'Is this what you needed the lab for?' I wasn't sure whether I had said the words or just thought them.

Violet was caressing the glass box that held an abomination. 'You have quaggas ...' she said.

I couldn't take my eyes off the glass chrysalis. 'That was an experiment, Violet. Hardly the same thing.' Finally I heard her inside voice: *You wouldn't understand. You've never wanted children.*

Ingrid sighed, limped to a chair, wheeled herself closer to the empty beakers, took one, poured whiskey from a hip flask into it.

'This is not a child, Violet. You lied to me! You said you were working. This is crazy!' I was yelling.

'And your little pet over there?' She pointed to the window behind Ingrid, where Donto was peering through the glass curiously.

'I was just experimenting ... you know what? I don't have to explain myself. Shut it down.'

Violet crossed her arms. 'No. He's mine.'

Ingrid's 'Jesus!' came just before the realisation of what Violet had actually done hit me.

The day she arrived, she asked if she could store samples in my cryo-freezer. 'Is your lab still up and running?' She sounded desperate. It was an odd way to greet a friend you hadn't seen in a long time. Nevertheless, I showed her the lab. The samples were the only thing she took with her when she got fired from her job. I remember feeling lost after the Baby A debacle; all I wanted was to be back at work. It was obvious that Violet wanted to continue working, just at her own pace and in a different setting. She didn't say what she was working on and I didn't ask – it didn't seem important. 'I lose my soul and they expect me to come back like nothing happened.' There was a quiet anger beneath the surface of her skin; every so often I would see rage flash under her cheeks and beneath her breastbone. 'My heart is breaking.' That's what she whispered as she ate everything I put in front of her – much to Ingrid's disgust. *Woah. Leave some for the dino dog, Starvacia.*

It was well after 10.00 p.m. when I heard her pleading: *I can't go back. I have nothing.* Like the prayers sinners say in church. I offered her a place to sleep for the night. After a week of tension, she and Ingrid finally got into it – it's what happens when opposites suddenly realise they are quite similar. 'You don't know anything about music, so shut up.' I had just come back from a run with Donto; whatever I was feeding was making him grow larger and he needed exercise as much as I did. The difference between the plants his ancestors ate and the versions I was feeding must have been what was making him so large. The dissension from the two women interrupted my thoughts about the quality of my soil versus that of the Jurassic period. 'I may not know about music, Ingrid, but I do know a washed-up rock star when I see one.' Ingrid's response came like lightning. 'Washed up? You're an unemployed scientist who is trying to hide the dry breast-milk stains on her cheap shirt.'

Donto growled, announcing our presence. 'Wow! I haven't seen a display like this since I watched those vintage reality TV shows about housewives.' Nobody answered me but I could hear them angrily muttering inside their heads, wishing unspeakable harm on each other.

Dinner was quiet until I suggested Violet move into one of the rondawels outside. 'It's a shame to leave them empty like that. Frank wouldn't have wanted his work to go to waste.' Violet faked gratitude. 'We get it. You loved your husband,' she said.

Ingrid glared at an empty space in front of her, determined not to make peace or show relief. 'I was once pregnant too, you know.' Both Violet and I stared at our plates. 'Oh please, don't feel sorry for me. I was happy ... I thought we were both happy. Can you imagine what the news billboards would have looked like? I had even planned my Bump Reveal outfit.' Violet picked up a braaied mealie and let her hands linger in front of her mouth like a car carelessly parked outside closed double garage doors. 'You don't know how little your joy means to someone until it threatens their livelihood. He was worried about a tour. MY BABY was a threat to tour money.' The slow crunching of mealie kernels in Violet's mouth filled the silence while Ingrid sipped her whiskey. 'I never saw it coming. Who would? He killed my child.' Ingrid made a pathetic sound that was supposed to be a laugh. 'Do you know how he did it?' Violet carried on chewing the same mouthful and I sliced my cold baked potato into smaller pieces. 'He shoved pills inside of me while we were making love and the next day I was sick and lost my baby. The doctor found traces of a white substance in my vagina. World's greatest couple – that's what people called us when we divorced. Motherfucker took half of all my shit.' Violet moved into the Blue Rondawel the next day.

'She did what?' Ingrid sounded truly horrified but we both ignored her. Violet kept her eyes on me, half expecting me to do something violent to her – or the thing she'd created.

   'I experiment with animals. This is something else, Vi. This is wrong.'

'You think you're so good because you stopped playing God, Nokuzola!' She was yelling and Ingrid looked surprised – she was convinced Violet's anger was only reserved for her. 'What the hell do you think you're doing here? Creating an oasis in the middle of the Karoo, bringing dead things back to life. How am I so different from you? Was I supposed to just accept that my baby died? Do you know what it's like to create something so beautiful and then have it taken away?'

My ears were burning and I was chasing air in and out of my lungs. 'I've made plenty of mistakes. I own my stuff, Violet! You've crossed a line and you know it.'

'Why does he look like that?' Ingrid asked, without a hint of humour or aggression.

For the first time, I took a good look at what's in the incubator. The baby's skin is thin, the tiny highways and freeways of veins visible on it. He looks to be about two years old but it's hard to tell because he's lying in a foetal position. 'I used the growth hormones in the lab ...' We all look where she is pointing. The bottle is labelled, in my writing, HGH (human growth hormone). Only I would know that it contains butterfly DNA – it's my lab and I know where everything is.

'I have never tested that on humans ...' My voice fades because there's a ringing in my ears.

'Does it look human to you?' Ingrid had meant to whisper that under her breath.

Untitled ii

Loud gasping, your own – that's what you wake up to. Then the chill sets in because you're beginning to feel again.

I felt my chest first. It felt like someone was trying to rip it in half. Every breath I took hurt. Everything is a blur because you've been frozen in a moment for years. The Pods were timelocked; the ship was on autopilot while we drifted away from Earth – Doctor Nguyen tells me it looked like a purple ball of smoke. She looks wistful when she says, 'We left so many people behind.' I'm hooked up to a machine monitoring my vitals when she says this. My heart rate starts racing and she looks at me with pity. It's a shared pity. Doctor Nguyen is the physiotherapist who helped me walk again – we all had to learn how to walk again. Except the Skeleton Crew – even though the ship was on autopilot some people had to stay 'awake' and prepare for the worst. 'They had no idea what was out here. So the brightest minds stayed awake and prepared for any eventuality.' Again she looks sad. It's been 20 years; she was a bright-eyed 25-year-old genius when she was secretly recruited by the Founders. I try to imagine my 14-year-old sister as a 34-year-old but I can't. Would she have grown her hair out? She always liked it short and during school holidays she would dye it a different colour. The last school holidays it was bright pink. Doctor Nguyen says the world was like a purple ball of smoke. Fourteen-year-old girls with short hair don't survive that kind of thing. So what's the use of trying to imagine Kamo as a 34-year-old?

'Space travel is not an exact science, folks. This is all new for us as well.'

The time locks were set to unlock in phases. The ships were able to fly manually for a while. After a year, the engineers and crew were unlocked and they started getting the ship ready and working out the logistics. We were unlocked next. Who is we? The 'young people'. I guess the plan was that we would acquire useful skills and training so when the Founders (people who financed this hell) were unlocked, we would be useful. The Founders were mainly people over the age of 60 – they were uber wealthy and had all kinds of ideas about a 'second youth' in space. None of us had aged, much to Annie's joy. Melanie was frozen for 20 years and she is still a whiney teenager – I guess some things are forever. The first few weeks of being awake were difficult; joints ached and the heartache was persistent. Earth was gone and so was my little sister.

Kamo had packed a Sesotho Bible in my bag. Every time I tried to read a few pages, anger wouldn't let me continue. Mme had written the Lord's Prayer on the back of the Bible.

Ntata rona ya mahodimong
lebitso la hao le ke le kgethehe
ho tle mmuso wa hao
thatho ya hao e etswe lefatsheng,
jwalokaha e etswa lehodimong.
O re fe kajeno bohobe ba rona ba tsatsi le leng le le leng
O re tshwarele melato ya rona,
Jwalokaha re tshwarela ba nang le melato ho rona
O se ke wa re isa melekong

O mpe ore lwele ho e mobe
Amen.

The Prayer is my daily mantra but for me it is not a prayer to God. It's a prayer to all those I left behind and those I miss. When the new world overwhelms me, I recite the prayer until my breathing is normal again and the pain in my chest disappears.

thatho ya hao e etswe lefatsheng, jwalokaha e etswa lehodimong
thy will be done on earth as it is in heaven

There were the X Cabins, which were really luxury apartments on Level 5 of the ship. X Cabins were for people who had made it into lists of magazines I'd never heard of – for being successful and wealthy, obviously. There was X-Annex meant for the 'support staff' of those families.

Annie and Jonty are not Cabin X people, nor are they X2 types. We live on Level 3 in Cabin X3. When I say 'we', I mean Melanie and I share a room and she's begun to treat me the way her parents did when she was a baby: 'Bonnie, could you make the baby a bottle? Bonnie, won't you be a love and load the washing machine?' I wasn't even 11 and Annie had found a way to make me Ma's cleaning assistant. While Ma was occupied with Melanie, a relative was looking after Baby Kamo. 'Bonnie, did you see my comic book? I was reading it last week.' 'Bonnie, please help me sew a button on.' 'I don't know how to do this, Bonnie.' 'Bonnie!' Bonnie?! I never once said it was okay to call me Bonnie. Not all those years ago and not even when we were floating far away from home where my little sister called me Bonolo – not some unwanted nickname.

The ship is large enough for me to get lost regularly, find someone to help me get back to where I need to be, and get lost again. I hardly ever feel like talking to anyone so I frequently get lost – sometimes on purpose. In the beginning there were days when I just sat on one of the many viewing decks and cried. My sister was dead and I didn't do anything to save her life. When our parents died, I promised never to let anything harm her – that's what family does. Most days on the ship I would just look out into the deep darkness around me and wonder why I was even alive. There was no sun to look at, no friends to visit, no family and no freedom. The library didn't have books that I wanted to read. The creator of this spaceship (and many others), Mr X, was a fan of Ayn Rand. Why else would there be 20 copies of each of her books in the library? Mr X was laughed at when he said that his spaceships would be like cruise liners in space. Every single spaceship that launched in the days before Fire Skies has a luxury cabin reserved for him. Just in case he decides to visit. The few South African books on the ship are the ones we were forced to read at school. I only spend time in the library to have quiet moments and read Kamo's favourite childhood books. She was a weird child who really enjoyed *The Gruffalo* – Jonty and Annie bought it as a Christmas present for us many years ago. She memorised the entire book so she would know if I was skipping pages to get out of reading to her.

> *O re fe kajeno bohobe ba rona ba tsatsi le leng le le leng*
> *Give us this day our daily bread*

Melanie talks about Kamo a lot. I sometimes forget that the two of them were like sisters, even though I was not close to the family. 'Remember when Kamo took one karate lesson and then beat up Jason Attwell?' Melanie did that all the time; she would step out of the shower and just start talking without checking if I was reading, sleeping or even in the room. I nodded and giggled because that was one of the only times I heard my father swear. I didn't even know he was a fan of the f-word. Melanie sighs and sits down on the bed next to me. 'What are we gonna do here for the rest of our lives, Bonnie?'

'Well, they've finally got the school situation sorted.'

'You should apply for a job with the engineering team.'

'And do what, Melanie?'

'I don't know … Discover things and actually live your life for you.'

O re tshwarele melato ya rona
And forgive us our trespasses

As much as I appreciate being alive, I don't think I can do it here on this ship, with all the baggage from my previous life. There is nothing on this ship for me. In a year we will 'dock'. Docking is when a couple of ships 'hang' in the same area to allow for inter-ship socialising. Support staff and those who don't have upper-level cabins are already being encouraged to 'volunteer' in the food gardens, sewing stations, entertainment ensembles, catering crews and playschools. Seems they had not anticipated how much work it actually takes to keep a ship of this size running smoothly. 'Volunteering' is not really what it says because some of the people who opted to stay in their cabins and not volunteer have found that their access to certain areas has been revoked. Security informed them that the Founding Cluster (another delightful new addition to our daily lives) felt it was unfair to those who were working to share privileges with those who didn't want to 'pull together for the greater good'. So, for the greater good, I've joined a group of mechanics and learned the ropes – or rather the tools. I discovered that there were Explorer Pods, small enough for one pilot and stocked with enough oxygen and intravenous minerals for a weeklong journey, and a first-aid kit. 'I guess they thought we would be much more adventurous,' laughed Keegan, my mechanic mentor. Those Pods keep me up at night. I ask Keegan a million questions about them until he lets me sit in one and shows me how everything works. So maybe I am just curious when I 'borrow' Keegan's code (I stand behind him when he punches it in every day).

O se ke wa re isa melekong
Lead us not into temptation

Melanie is snoring and I want a walk because sleep was playing hide and seek with me. Why am I walking to the garage where the Explorer Pods are parked? Keegan's code opens the giant doors and I decide that 'docking date' is too far off and I need to leave now. Surely they won't miss one Explorer Pod? At least then Melanie will have her room to herself – plus, Annie and Jonty can stop worrying about me. Maybe when I'm out there I will find a different set of people with a sense of history and irony, because this place is suffocating me. Keegan showed me how to 'suit up'. A few minutes before I pull the small lever that opens the garage door, I wonder if this is what Kamo wanted for me. Maybe I don't deserve to be here but my sister believed that I deserved a second chance at life. Who am I to disappoint her?

> *O mpe ore lwele ho e mobe*
> *But deliver us from evil*

I didn't know where to go (no roads or highways in space) so I just chose a direction and let the pod do the rest. The silence in the pod and the darkness around me lulled me to sleep. For the first time since I woke up in space, I actually slept for the, impossible Earth standard, eight hours. I didn't think about the fuel problem until the dashboard started talking to me. It was the Afrikaans woman from the airport hangar. Interesting choice of voice; I don't hate it. How on earth can we still be relying on fuel even this far away from Earth? Maybe I should have asked Keegan about fuel but I was too busy fantasising about being an explorer.

The dashboard tells me there's 'an unidentified planet' nearby where I can 'dock'. That doesn't seem like the best plan, but what else am I supposed to do? In primary school, my science teacher once told us about objects floating in space forever. That thought scares me enough to let the Pod land itself on the 'unidentified planet'.

Six pairs of feet – at least that's what it looks like – are approaching the Pod. If I stay inside will it seem hostile? Is it safer just to stay inside? Why didn't I ask Keegan about weapons or shields? My instincts are telling me to just get out of the Pod. If I'm wrong ... I'll deal with that when it happens.

I exit the Pod slowly with my hands in the air (who knew TV would teach me so much?). I'm breathing so fast that my helmet is misting up. Through the fog of my breath I see something that literally makes my legs go weak. I fall on my knees, still keeping my hands in the air. How is this possible? Standing around me, all with their hands up is ... me. Not really me; but there are six people or things standing around with the same face as me. Freckles in all the right places and the two tiny moles under their left eyes. They are different heights and sizes but all wearing the same Me mask. I drop my hands to my sides and they drop theirs as well. Oh God!

The Colourful

The High Heel Killer

'The High Heel Killer.' What a stupid name. I hate it. These media clowns aren't even trying. If I had studied journalism, like I wanted to, 'High Heel Killer' would never have made it into print. Blood is surprisingly thin. The kind I've been dealing with since I was 12 is thick ... but Ray-Ban Guy's blood was thin, messy and unexpectedly hot. Who knew? Mme's lawyer convinced the judge that I don't have any money, so I wouldn't run away. That's all that I could make out; my brain had become a sieve. There was some mention of me never having broken any laws, psychiatric evaluation and assurance that I would not kill anyone else (my interpretation). The last bit was funny (inappropriate). Mme's boyfriend paid my bail and then asked me, as I was getting out of his car, to please keep my distance. 'This is hard on her too, just stay away for a while.' From his insipid mouth to reality; I haven't left my room since I stepped out of the car. It's been weeks.

Weeks. Months. Years. How long had I been following a map of confusion, fear and anger? Three years. I spent those years walking myself into the concrete and tar of the city. How many steps did I walk trying to get to the taxi rank, to work, from work to a taxi, from that taxi to another taxi rank and back home again? How many afternoons had I heard the Ray-Ban Guy trying to convince people to buy his cheap knock-off sunglasses? People really liked him; I found him corny – in fact, I was pretty sure people only laughed because it was part of their routine. He was always ready with a joke and a story about why a certain pair of glasses would suit you.

'Why did you kill that man?' Doppelgangers of that question confronted me. Mme didn't even look at me when she asked it. She sighed heavily. Heavily like when I told her that a hand from a sea of bodies in town touched my breast. I was 12. She asked angrily if I recognised the person who did it. We were in the

CBD, people were pushing past us and I knew the person who did it was walking away happily unpunished. 'Did he hurt you?' I looked at my feet.

My feet were complaining. It was the taxi driver's fault; I asked him if I was taking the right taxi. 'Hey, S'dudla, you're making me late. Just get in.'

The roads became unfamiliar and I knew for sure that I was headed in the opposite direction to where I needed to be. Asking if this was a different route got me kicked out. 'Voetsek!' is all I heard when a sniggering passenger closed the door.

It was far away from the taxi rank in town and my shoes were threatening me. Wearing high heels was a stupid idea; I should have listened to Tshepo.

Tshepo was outside the door. No more words, just the shuffling of feet, plastic bags of food, and a sigh. In the beginning, it was forced syrupy words of encouragement. The anger was expected: 'If you don't want to see me, say so. People say I shouldn't come see you because you're a fucking killer. I'm wasting my time.' I remember those words because it was the first time I saw what was actually making my sides hurt. In front of the mirror I stood topless, looking at white bits of bone-like stubs sticking out from where my ribs were. My boyfriend's anger was my only witness.

Witness the city turn against us! There were many potential witnesses: Ray-Ban Guy, Aus' Maneo who sells braaied mealies in the morning, school kids who constantly argue about artists I've never heard of ... Why then did I feel so frightened when I realised the conversation behind me was about me? The two male voices slapped city sounds away from my ears like a mother does when her child reaches for the pots before supper is ready. It wasn't menacing at all; their voices were casual: 'Those thighs ... I'm going first ... Let's see how far she goes ... Ha, probably walking to her car ... Two for one.' Why did I turn around and look? They both smiled, laughed and then crossed the road. The tall one turned back: 'Ne re dlala, sester'. A joke ...

'A joke?'

'Yeah, he was probably joking.' That was the last time I accepted a lift from my colleague Phillipa. She was distracted and took the wrong turn two blocks away from the taxi rank. 'He says things like that all the time to women at the office. He means nothing by it. You'll get used to it – I did. He's married anyway.' I opened the door and pushed one foot out. 'This isn't your stop. Let me make a U-turn and drop you off closer.' Maybe I declined, the memory is foggy. Pain does that: it overtakes your flow of thought with force. And I was angry and in pain.

Pain wakes me up. It is unbearable in the mornings. Thankfully, there is not a lot of blood on the sheets. Should there be a lot of blood? Boiled water and Dettol is all that's available for the open wounds. Mme trusted it for childhood injuries. It was both an antibacterial and a threat. 'You are going to have marks on your legs. Who wants to marry a woman with marks on her legs? Those boys you climb trees with must marry you! Aaargh, just go and get the Dettol.'

This was funny until my period came with its luggage and strict instructions from Mme who treated me like a frail prisoner. The sun became my prison guard. Mme was an irrational warden. 'I had to take a bus because there was a taxi strike, Mme.' 'I said to be home before dark. You think you're the boss now? Boys will ruin your life. You don't know everything.'

Everything hurt, it was difficult to breathe. The bone-like stubs were getting longer. I killed Ray-Ban Guy and now my body is turning against me. While in the holding cell, my shoulder was on fire. It hurt just to lean against the wall. The policeman was not rough when he put the handcuffs on. Maybe the injury was from his knee on my back as he pinned me down on the ground. I didn't run. Why? Because I only had one good shoe on. I sat on the floor next to Ray-Ban Guy and waited for the police to arrive (they were always nearby in the CBD). One shoe still on and the other, bloody, in my hand. 'My shoe is ruined,' is what I said, according to the newspapers. I heard my neighbour wondering (loudly) whether living next door to a killer was safe.

'Safe?'

'Yes.'

'I don't think I understand what you're saying.'

'Do you feel safe here?' I asked again slowly. Tshepo handed me a drink and we walked outside to check on our meat. 'Why wouldn't I feel safe here?' He looked around with mock shock. 'People are buying meat, braaing, having drinks and listening to music.'

'Yes but that woman was raped here a few weeks ago,' I said, eyeing my beer. He sighed with no drama. 'It was by the toilets, not here ... Wasn't she drunk anyway?'

The guy braaing our meat signalled that it was almost ready. 'I don't know if she was drunk but I don't feel …'

His laughter cut me off. 'Nawe uthand' ukuba dramatic. You don't get messy drunk.' He got up to fetch our meat. 'Besides, you're with me, nobody will touch you.'

'You need to see her again.' Mme sounded tired. She wanted me to see the psychiatrist who was going to testify that I had had some kind of mental break. 'She says you have never done anything like this before. You're strong. This is not you. People like … liked you. My mother's aunt was sick. She can help prove that you're sick too.' Mme works at the canteen of a psychiatric hospital. She has been working there for many years.

Mme is one of those people who will remember everyone's names, doctors and patients alike, and memorise facts about them. 'Naledi was upset that there was no spinach today. She's the one with the eating disorder and a brother who is a priest.' I wonder how Mme would describe me to her boyfriend if I was a patient. 'You know that girl I told you about? The one who murdered a guy at a taxi rank? She eats a lot of butternut and the backs of her shirts are always bloody.'

Bloody was followed by waxy. Waxy was followed by the

impossible. I looked in the mirror and cried. It was the first time I had cried since I hit a man with my shoe with so much force that it pierced the soft skin of his neck and he bled all over me and the pavement. I didn't gasp or cry then. People around me screamed and gasped, others ducked to avoid blood spray and some were frozen in shock. I sat down next to Ray-Ban Guy and hugged my shoe. His feet were doing a little dance, and then nothing. There were people watching me; some in shock, others cursing me with their eyes; a few asked me questions I couldn't hear over the sound of my heartbeat. That was supposed to be the only impossible thing to happen to me. But here I am, becoming the inexplicable now.

'Now why are you walking like that?' I turned around to see Ray-Ban Guy smiling. There was nothing to smile about. I had walked six blocks in new shoes, tripped but didn't fall when I finally got to my destination, and there he was having fun at my expense. I ignored him and took two more successful steps before I fell flat on my face in a puddle of pavement water. The words were loud. Loud enough for me to hear but not for the whole city to hear; the city that hated me, assaulted me with sound, violence and smells. I'd been so close to getting into the right taxi, so that I could be enveloped in the safety of my tiny room. He didn't have to say what he did, but he did.

Did I even know it was wings? Why was I expecting feathers like that of a chicken? Firm, shiny, black feathers like a cape on my shoulders and back. Once they sprouted I knew that impossible was just a matter of experience. Wings with tips down to my ankles. A clerk at the court spat 'monster' when I walked past her (in handcuffs). I am a monster. A beautiful monster with wings and no fear for the first time in my life. Nobody would ever understand this.

This back room is the only place I could afford on my laughable salary that is nothing but a glorified transport budget. It is one of three rooms in an old lady's backyard. The old lady is Mam' Mahlangu and she is only interested in us paying our rent on time. She was a widow who kept to herself; the shops and church were the only things that made her leave her house. Sometimes I would offer to get her a few things if I was on my way to the shops. She had the look of someone who was used to being alone and unaccustomed to kindness. When I returned from jail and my shoulders were itchy and hot, she knocked on my door and handed me a sjambok and a first-aid kit. 'The world is a dangerous place,' she said soberly and walked away quietly.

Quietly is how I did it. I dusted myself off and picked up the shoe that I had fallen out of. There was no wild animal scream from me as my hand moved up and down, landing sharp blows with the heel. When instinct kicked in and Ray-Ban Guy decided to fight back, the heel had already won. 'Ulayekile!' That's what he said before I fell. Who was he to determine what I did and didn't deserve? The same city that reduced him to a con artist had beaten me and he thought I deserved it. He laughed and said 'ulayekile'. He shouldn't have said it.

It is beautiful from up here, the cruel city and all the people walking its streets at night. Why did I never look up at these beautiful old rotting buildings? I was so busy counting my steps and craving invisibility. The wings are strong although I almost fell to my death a few times (who's going to give me flying lessons?). I birthed myself; it was bloody and painful but now I'm standing on the roof of a city as something new.

Up here nobody can tell me what I deserve, who I should be or how to be. And I dare those down below to open their mouths and tell another tired, underpaid woman that she deserves the cruelty of the city. I'm the enemy of cruelty and they'll have to deal with me.

Once Upon a Town

It was in a gutter when he first saw her, mouth inelegantly clasped around the spine of a rat. She was a terrible feeder then – not that she's got better now. 'You're going to scare the other kids,' he shouted. She turned around and used her left foot to scratch the back of her right leg, mouth still attached to the giant rat. 'Do you want to start a new trend, meisie?' Her eyes were interested in the conversation but her mouth was busy. 'Ja. A trend. These kids are always looking for a new high.' Phatu felt the rat grow limp and threw it at the boy's feet with a growl that was more puppy than wild animal. 'I know what you are,' he said, attempting to reassure her that he meant her no harm, but it came out sounding like a threat.

If 'love at first sight' is a thing you believe in, dear reader, then this was it. They were both 12 when the giant sewer rat lost its life in the streets of a city by the sea. Phatu still hadn't got used to the salty blood she was living on but at least the livestock in her village was safe. Petyr was his name. Yes, with a Y – because his mother had always been obsessed with Russians and the ballet.

Petyr's mother was a dark-skinned girl from Mitchells Plain who dreamed of pirouetting her way out of poverty. What did the world do, to be deprived of a born dancer who would never see the world stage, let alone the ballet classes that the pastor's wife used to organise? Her gait parted crowds – in church, at school, even at the small corner shop; people in her neighbourhood just wanted to watch the way her legs moved. The boys would wait for her to get off the train and shout, 'Petro-neh-la, I love you!' She only smiled once she had her back to them; ballet remained her only love.

When there was a ballet on at the big theatre in town, she would stand across the street from it and imagine herself on stage on opening night. The interior of the theatre was a mystery to her but imagination doesn't need reality for it to flourish. Unfortunately, all she ended up doing was cleaning other people's clothes and homes until every demi plié became a bow to those who paid her. Once she became a mother she made sure Petyr was in ballet lessons from age four. Nothing was going to stop his mother from making it to Russia with her tiny dancer. (Who cared if he didn't want to live in Russia? Who cared if Russia didn't want him?)

Phatu lived in a small village with her father, a man with very few cows but who harboured ambitions of gaining more cattle from the family of the man who would marry his daughter. He sent her to the best school a few kilometres outside of the village. It was most convenient for him because he couldn't be bothered with raising a child. Had he known that laying with many women would one day result in one of them leaving a baby at his doorstep, with a note saying 'this is what your love gave me', he would have given them a fake address. Besides the advantage of not having to be an active parent if his daughter went to school, he also knew that an educated daughter meant he could request more cows from his future in-laws. That's what people in the cities were doing now, demanding more money for educated daughters – he didn't make or change the rules. Neighbours always spoke about what a kind man he was for sparing no expense for his daughter's education, much to his delight.

All was going according to plan until she was sent home from boarding school because she was ill. She complained about dry eyes, insomnia and inability to keep any food down. Her ailments were affecting her academic performance and keeping her out of class. The principal, rightfully, sent her home. With a child who seemed to be wasting away, the man was growing desperate but didn't ask for anyone's help; his daughter grew weak and pale. In her body, Phatu felt like her insides were melting; occasionally she would spit up what tasted like bile. Because she was sensitive to light and he had cattle to look after, her father would take her out on the stoep, for fresh air and to avoid bedsores, in the evenings. It worked for him because her eyes didn't see the sun and his neighbours couldn't use theirs to see what had become of Phatu. Otherwise, the rumours would have grown legs and run wild through the village. A wild rumour had a way of lingering in the minds of people, even if it had been dispelled.

Most assumed she was still at school – why would a child waste an opportunity to release her family from poverty? Phatu was going to be the first person in her family to finish high school and graduate from university. Education was important, even if children didn't like going to school. But instead of working on releasing her family from poverty, Phatu was sitting on the stoep

155

propped up by a continental pillow. A lamb was bleating nearby; her father always had a favourite that he would let follow him everywhere – he used to be like that with her too. Perhaps she was slowly giving in to her melting insides but Phatu heard what she thought was a heartbeat. It wasn't close enough to be her own but it was near enough. The lamb in front of her seemed to be vibrating; it smelled like freshly cut grass which made her mouth water. Surely the disease is finally finishing me off, she thought as she dragged herself up onto all fours. She was saying her good-byes under her breath when she suddenly couldn't hear her voice anymore. The slurping and sucking was the only audible thing. Phatu didn't hear the agonised sound made by the tiny lamb struggling under her strengthening grip, or her father's yelling.

It was love at first sight, if you believe in that kind of thing. She showed him her hiding place: an abandoned zoo next to a university campus – right in the middle of the city. The city is like that: it loves new and shiny things, which also leads it to be a graveyard of previously beautiful relics. The zoo was abandoned in the 80s and bricked up once authorities realised that it had become an illegal little suburb, next to a real leafy suburb, for those without homes. Phatu spent weeks removing bricks strategically so that she could live there without attracting the attention of other homeless people, students looking for privacy, the police or rich people who lived down the road from the zoo. 'How did you break through the bricks and cement?' Petyr asked. She liked that he sounded impressed. 'I punched the bricks,' she said. He believed her and she knew it. 'Do you know this place was built by an old colonist who wanted animals from all over the world?' Petyr said, looking around at how neatly she had her things packed in the corner of what was once the lion's cage.

'Yeah. He was a murderer who wanted a menagerie.'

Before long they had made some kind of home with guinea fowls and two pigs (stolen off a truck as a practical joke on Valentine's Day) as pets. Their days were spent dodging the light between the tall buildings of the city. Petyr danced at traffic lights for money and Phatu kept an eye out for police or someone who had already claimed that traffic light as their territory. Evenings were quiet and mostly spent in their roofless home. That is how they grew up – alongside each other, never feeling like an 'other' but just right.

When they lay quietly gazing at the stars, she would trace the homemade tattoos on his neck and ask if he knew he would get bitten.

'Are you jas?'

That always made her laugh. He'd always made her laugh, since the day they met. Who could have imagined that the gang was also a pack? They are so similar, those two words, but rarely the same thing. 'Why do you always ask me that?' he turned to look at her.

'Because you actually know why you are the way you are, but I don't know if I was born this way or not.'

'Does it matter?'

'Yes and no.' She hid her face in the hoodie he gave her. He was afraid of her sometimes, the way her eyes glistened at night and how strong she was becoming. Phatu was spending more time in the sun and seemed to be growing immune to its sting, although she continued to wear a hoodie and covered her face with a bandana, 'like a G' she would say, guffawing. She diligently tracked the phases of the moon and made sure that the cage at the abandoned zoo by the university was ready in time. Nothing and nobody else would have been able to keep him in that cage; she was the only one who could. While he howled and whined, she would dance the way he'd taught her when they were younger and sing his favourite song. She never tired of the routine. When she got tired of singing she would sit down and tell him a story – his favourite. He would then devour whatever small animal she'd locked him in with; Pavlovian reaction.

The story was about a little boy whose mother was born a dancer in a world where dancing was prohibited for girls like her. She met a man on a train, a tap dancer. Walked home with him and gave herself to him. He thought himself irresistible, but really she saw a dancer child in her future. Once was all it took and very soon she was dreaming of a ballerina with hair gelled down and a pink tutu. Out came a little boy with curly hair and deep-brown eyes. 'No matter. Boys can dance too.' And so she gave him a Russian name and played only music composed by Russian maestros. Little Boy With Russian Name was well on his way to becoming the ballet star his mother dreamed of, attending ballet classes from a young age – he was a light in a dark place. That was his problem … Not HIS problem but that of the light. Things that lurk in the shadows do not like the light. People get used to one tiny light and begin to seek out more of it in the world and in themselves – that's how the light liberates us. What becomes of the dark and its denizens, when others keep lighting up the world?

The Pack In The Dark sought out Little Boy With Russian Name, enticing him with gifts at first. He declined and held tightly onto his light. If he wasn't going to give up the light willingly, they would take it forcefully. And forcefully they did, with a kidnapping and teeth to his limbs – so that he could morph into one of them. For days his mother searched for the light of her life. The entire neighbourhood did – who could have stolen their light? Days were dark when he was assumed missing, dead or worse. Then the worst happened: he appeared one day – a dying light in the dark. He was now one of them – revelling in the violence of the night. His mother dared to defy her fear and claim back Little Boy With Russian Name but he was too far gone for her to reach.

Phatu dragged out the story for as long as she could. It was at this point that Petyr, with long claws, hairy chest and hair slicked back from sweat, would growl (still not quite human): 'Why didn't he go with her? What happened to him in the end?' The sun would have begun rising, the blood on his mouth drying; his light was returning and the question was always the same. Even at this point, Phatu wouldn't open the gate to the enclosure. The hair on his limbs would have to fall off first, and only then was it safe to release him. 'I don't know. Why do you think he didn't go with his mother?' Phatu asked, knowing not to expect an answer. She got up to get water so he could clean the blood off his face, chest and hands. In the cage, Petyr whined and growled. 'The light was too much for him, that's why. They all looked to him. He was the only light in the dark. It was burning him.'

Untitled iii

My mother calls me Hailee – it's her idea of a joke. 'The skies turned black and you fell out of the sky. Like hail ... Get it? Ha ha ha. My little Hailee.'

My mother's name is Millicent. That's it. No second name or surname. As if to add more confusion – and take away more letters – she prefers to be called Sente. Pronounced Se-n-te, like the money. You know, a cent. 'I came into this world with nothing. Not even sente entsho. Call me Sente.' She jokes about coming into this world without so much as a 'black cent' but she never says where she's from or how she and Yaaseen survived the Fire Rain.

We joke a lot about not having a surname. Surnames are Old World things. So is giving birth. Sente found me and cared for me until I could walk again, so she is my mother. There are a few others living in the rubble of what used to be Johannesburg. We live in a penthouse at the abandoned (even before fire fell from the sky) Carlton Hotel on the 30th floor. No roof over our heads but we live in a penthouse. The top of the building was probably blown away in the last days. We don't talk about the last days. There isn't much to say. Too much lost and so many blank spaces.

One day the world was dull and the next it was filled with far too much excitement and panic. One morning, while we were eating sandwiches at break time, Melanie asked me if I thought we would see the sun again. 'We can feel it, Mel. It hasn't gone anywhere. There's just ...'

'I know.' Her bottom lip looked like it was going to fall on the ground. 'But do you think those clouds will ever move? Satellites can't see Earth; there haven't been any clear pictures ... I'm scared.'

Melanie was my half-sister; sister because we were inseparable as kids and half because my mother cleaned her father's house, so perhaps they half considered me a part of their family. After my parents died in a car accident, Melanie's parents promised to look after my sister and me – my real sister, Bonolo. I guess her having that name is a joke too. Bonolo means 'easy' or 'uncomplicated' but nothing, except her birth, was easy for my sister. Bonolo was a child genius who got straight As, went to university before her age mates, graduated and never became the engineer she wanted to be. Instead, she grew tired of the job rejection letters and ended up working as a secretary for a GP. She had also decided that being smart was a disadvantage so she played small and unremarkable until she started to believe it.

Sente thinks I don't like talking about Bonolo but that's not true. Bonolo is the one thing that makes me feel sane. She is like a light I run to in my mind when the new world causes clouds in my heart. When I'm staring up at the new sky, I run to Bonolo. Sometimes I find her in the kitchen of our small, four-roomed house and watch her eating supper quietly, her one hand scooping up pap and gravy, the other hovering over my homework. Whenever she spotted a mistake she would look up at me and pretend to choke on her food. At other times I run to Bonolo and find her sleeping peacefully on the sofa, after a long day of work. Quiet moments with my sister are why the silence of the new world doesn't scare me. I've grown used to the Green skies that turn Purple at night.

'Seentaaaaaaaaay! Your baby is awake. She's alliiiiiive!' Those were the first words I heard. It was Yaaseen. I couldn't see him at first so I tried to sit up but my arms wouldn't move. Suddenly a bearded face appeared, looking down at me. He said, 'Sorry, it's the straps. You were like a trout on a boat.' He unfastened the straps and helped me sit up while my brain was catching up with who or what I was. Instinctively I brought a hand up to my eye and Yaaseen slapped it away; he looked nervous. 'Sentaaaaaaaaay. Please come here … NOW!' The word 'Now' jolted a picture out of the fog in my mind. 'Bo … Bonol … Bonolo.' The rest is still foggy but I remember that I didn't speak for weeks. What was there to say? Yaaseen and Sente didn't push me. They spoke to me like I would one day choose to answer them. They looked at me when they spoke to me, said my new name when addressing me and life carried on around me. We sat together at the dinner table; they went 'shopping' for clothes they thought I would like, taught me how to walk again and cleaned the wound where my left eye used to be. I avoided my own reflection and walked the dark, damp rooms of the abandoned hotel when the penthouse got too small for three people.

We were a weird trio. Yaaseen was slim, very tall and his broad shoulders were always hunched. Must have been a way to make people feel comfortable around him. (My sister Bonolo was also tall and she hunched her shoulders in the same kind of way, especially around a boy she liked.) Sente looked like an old woman, a little soft in the belly and skin that was beginning to sag. Although she seemed to be in her 60s, she behaved a lot like a child. Sometimes when she was making supper, she would stop. Throw the food out the window and start making a brand-new meal. And then there was me with my bandaged eye, neglected afro and bouts of silence and anxiety.

It took me a few days to figure out why I was always anxious – there was no People Noise. No cars, no radios, no conversations, no music and no background to our new world. We were the background, the foreground, the main focus and that which is out of focus. It was exhausting to know that we were it. *You can be angry but you're not allowed to keep quiet, Kamo. It's just the two of us. Who else must I talk to? Do you want me to go crazy and talk to myself?* That's what Bonolo would say whenever we had had a falling out and I chose to punish her with silence. Yaaseen only spoke to himself when he thought we were watching him. His solo conversations were nonsensical and occasionally funny. Really, he seemed to be watching Sente and I wanted to know why. I had to wait until he was helping me with physio and Sente was out doing whatever it was she did when she said 'going shopping'.

'Yaaseen?'

'Yes, Hailee? Please tell me your real name, man. Can't be nice to be called some junk name all the time.'

'Kamo. Kamogelo.' The last person to say my name was my sister. Hearing it caused a lump in my throat but I carried on. 'Is Yaaseen your real name?' He nodded and carried on helping me stretch. 'I know you're not crazy,' I told him.

'Never said I was.'

'Why do you look at Sente like …'

'Like I don't trust her?' He stood up and wiped his brow. 'How many women over 60 do you think can walk up and down the stairs of this old skyscraper once a week? Why did I wind up here in this building?'

He was sweating and I was getting anxious but I let him speak. Some of it was difficult to follow but it sounded like Yaaseen was in the middle of a long operation, on a patient with cancer, when fire started falling from the heavens. 'There was chaos in the hospital. I hid inside one of our labs … I don't know what I was thinking.' He woke up in the penthouse and Sente's explanation was that she was looking for survivors and found him in the streets.

'Why is that so hard to believe?' I asked, pulling myself up onto my feet.

'Hail … Kamo … I live … lived … in Kimberley. I was in a hospital in Kimberley. That's more than 400 kilometres from here.' His voice echoed in such an eerie way that we both kept quiet for a while.

Yaaseen walked back towards me and touched my face, 'Aren't you curious about what she did to your eye?'

We both rushed to the mirror in the bathroom and stared at my reflection. I looked older. There were parts of my face that looked familiar but I was not me in many ways. Nothing was the same so why did I expect my face to have stayed as it was in the old world?

Yaaseen looked at me, asking for permission to remove the bandage. I nodded and exhaled, trying to keep the tears away. I kept both my eyes closed until Yaaseen said, 'I have to pull the eyelids apart on the eye.' The room smelled like antiseptic and skin that hadn't been aired in a while. I heard him leave, walk back in and then felt a wet cloth on my left eye. 'Am I hurting you?' I shook my head and held my breath. 'Okay. Open your eyes.'

Yaaseen gasped and covered his mouth. I tried to blink away

the blurriness then turned around to take a look at myself in the mirror. My entire eyeball was black. I tried to scream but it got caught in my throat. 'What the ...' Letters appeared on the mirror and I stopped talking out of shock.

WELCOME, SUBJECT A.

'Who is Subject A, Yaaseen?'

'What?!' He looked genuinely confused. I pointed at the mirror, 'That's what it says there.' He looked at me the way Bonolo looked at me when I once asked her how I would know if I was ready for sex. 'There's nothing there.'

CHECKING VITALS.

'You don't see anything about vitals? On the mirror?'

'No.'

I turned around to look at him and there was writing on his forehead: SUBJECT C. Yaaseen put his hand over my left eye and asked, 'Can you see the writing now?' It was gone. He removed his hand and more writing came up. It was too much text and I felt dizzy. I blinked hard and it went away. 'I think it's my eye.'

We heard a door close and Sente's voice drifting towards us: 'Can you believe I saw a rhino on Plein Street? I didn't think any of the ...' She stopped talking when she saw the two of us standing in the bathroom. She sighed and closed her eyes, like my real mother used to do before she gave me a lecture. Yaaseen ran to the door and shut it in her face. With his back against the door, he looked at me and said, 'Can your eye find us a way out of here?'

Nthatisi

The banging has stopped but I know they, whoever *they* are, are not gone. They must be working on Plan B; if Mom's letter is to be believed, they won't stop till they have me too. I really wish Dad hadn't moved to Dubai – he would be home with me right now. He worked from home before the divorce and was always home when I came back from school. Sometimes he would wait for me at the bus stop and then we would go get kotas together. Of course I would think about food at a time like this. This was supposed to be a fairly boring Friday and now I'm locked in a secret room above Mom's bedroom. Surely this can't be real? Am I having a dissociative episode? Is that what it's even called? I should have paid attention when Mpumi was watching that documentary on serial killers.

These people have Ma and I don't know what to do. She said I'll know what to do but I don't. I'm just a 15-year-old. The letter didn't even make sense. I need to read it again while the banging on the door has stopped. Hopefully the neighbours will see something is wrong; Mam' Jela knew when I started smoking behind the house. Where is she now? Typical! She also saw me kissing her nephew and practically camped outside waiting for Mom to come home. Now I'm stuck here with a letter and a box of strange things that don't make sense and not a sign of her.

Nthati

If you got the SOS message – GET THE BOX UNDER MY BED AND READ THE LETTER NOW – on your device then it means they have taken me. I'm sorry your phone is dead. The SOS is also a virus that I (got one of the geeks at work to install) activated remotely. Can't risk someone tracking you. That SOS is the last message you'll get on that phone. Chuck it! I'm so sorry, my girl. This was not supposed to happen – I didn't believe the stories myself. It was just a silly story … tshomo. You wouldn't know any because I never told them to you.

Nthati, you are in danger and I cannot help you … Nobody can. If you're going to make it, I need you to understand one very important thing – this letter is the only thing you can trust. You're going to get messages from my number or even hear me calling out for you. It is NOT me. It may sound like me or be a message from my phone number but it is not me. No matter how scared you are, even if you see me in the street or in a car – HA SE NNA.

This is the worst thing a mother could possibly ask of a child but I need you to make your way to Lesotho and find my cousin, your Uncle Mohau. He hasn't seen you since you were a baby but he will be expecting you (he's the only member of the family who still believes the prophecy). He

will know what to do. I'm so sorry, my baby. Let
me try to explain as quickly as I can.

When I was a little girl, my mother used to
tell me ditshomo (folk stories). Every night it
was a different one with a different lesson until
she began telling me the same story over and
over. The story of a little girl named Tselane.
TLDR (did I do that right? You said it means
Too Long Didn't Read so I'm going to summa-
rise). Tselane's mother was working in the fields
so she was left home alone. This was during a
time when (cannibal) giants existed and chickens
could still talk (don't laugh, Nthati, this is serious). Because of the threat of giants, Tselane's
mother made up a song that her daughter would
recognise and know to open the door. It was a
password of sorts. A loathsome giant was passing
by and he heard the song so the next day he sang
it. Tselane was too smart for him and told him
that he didn't sound like her mother. Ledimo
(the giant) went home and swallowed a hot iron

rod (don't question this, just keep reading) and it
transformed his voice — he sounded exactly like
Tselane's mother. He went back, sang the song;
Tselane was fooled, so she opened the door and
Ledimo kidnapped her, threw her in a sack and
made his way home. He was going to eat her for
supper and this pleased him.

There are many different versions of how the girl
was saved. Most of them involve alcohol and a
sack of snakes and bees. The ending is what you
need to know. This is the ending my mother used
to tell me. While being stung by bees and bitten
by snakes, Ledimo ran to the river. Because his
eyes had been stung, he accidentally immersed
his head in the muddy riverbank, where he
turned into a tree.

What does this have to do with you and me? We
are descendants of the Tselane in the story. This is
something my mother told me when I eventually
asked her why she kept telling me the same story

over and over. It seems there is a prophecy that descendants or followers of Ledimo will one day come and find the daughter of Tselane's people. They are basically a cult of cannibals who believe that by eating the heart of a daughter of Tselane, they will bring their father (Ledimo) back. I want to say it's nonsense, but you're reading the letter so it's got to be true.

Ledimo's people have been searching for our bloodline for many years. I wrote this letter after Mohau contacted me and told me that he had been hearing rumours about cannibals in Lesotho who were making their way to Soweto to find a daughter of their enemy before she turns 16. That was a few months before your 15th birthday. Mohau made me write this letter and put together the box with your passport, money and things that won't make sense to you now.

They are masters of disguise, these cannibals, which is why it's important not to believe anything but this letter. Again, if you hear my voice, get a message from me or even see me in the streets, RUN! There are names and addresses of people who will help you get to Lesotho safely. The password is 'Ba re ene ere' — that is what you say at the beginning of ditshomo. I honestly can't believe I'm writing this but if this really happens I want you to know what to do. When you finally get to Lesotho you have to say these words to Mohau: 'E aba ke tshomo ka ma thetho.' This is what the storyteller says when he or she is done telling ditshomo. That is the only way Mohau will know it's really you. The people who are after you are very good at pretending to be other people. Mohau has probably encountered many of them pretending to be me or you. The password is very important, Nthati. Don't forget it! It is the only way you can get the help you need to get.

Nthatisi, there's one more thing: you have to get to Lesotho and stay there until your birthday.

Mohau and his wife will keep you safe until you turn 16. Don't worry about me. I named you Nthatisi for selfish reasons. I knew people would call me Mmanthatisi (Mother of Nthatisi). Mmanthatisi is another one of our rebel ancestors. She was a queen (regent) who led armies and kept her people, the Batlokwe, alive in awful times. Being your mother has made me feel brave and I hope that I have been a good mother to you.

PS: There is a secret room above my bedroom (see the drawing). There is a way to escape from there, should you need to.

PPS: The Red Cloak has been in our family for a long time. My grandmother gave it to me when I got married. She said it would shield (make invisible) the wearer from her enemies. Keep it on while you're travelling. In case you're wondering ... Yes, she of the Red Hood was apparently a close friend of (our ancestor) Tselane. We have a lot to talk about.

Last thing (I promise): There is a book in there that will give you answers when you're lost. You are not to show this book to anyone. It is written in Sesotho – I don't feel so silly for making you learn to read and write it now.

I love you and I'm sorry that I'm not there to help you. I believe in you. You're amazing, my baby. Don't worry about me, I will find my way back to you. See you soon.

Mmanthatisi

'That's all there is, there isn't any more.'

– Ethel Barrymore

Acknowledgements

There are so many people I would like to thank. This collection is something I've wanted to do for a long time but I allowed fear to be a dream stealer. *Intruders* wouldn't exist if it wasn't for the encouragement of Marcia Shange and Andrea Nattrass – thank you both. Ma aka the best storyteller in the world: Thank you so much for giving me stories, storytelling and love. Pa: Thanks for always reminding me that I am capable and worthy. Junior: I know you were searching for your name here (he he). I love you, Jooneeeee! The rest of my family: Thank you for being the best hype-team of all time. Nomali Minenhle Cele: Remember 5 million years ago when we were both dreaming about UJU and by-lines? UJU is the place I delivered 'Manoka'; thank you for always believing in the words. Muneera Davids: Thanks for Science Eyeing a story for me. Richard Sherman: 'On the Run' would be dull if you hadn't shared that crazy story. Thanks to you and Jill for making your home a safe space when I needed a break from *Intruders*. Sipho Hlongwane: Thanks for asking me to write a short story for that *Mail & Guardian* supplement – 'The High Heel Killer' is still one of my favourite stories. Zakes Mda: We need to celebrate this collection at Ntate Mahlangu's place in Stellenbosch, BFF. Thank you for always making time for me. I love you. Lauren Beukes: Remember when you told me not to 'give my word babies away for free'? I didn't and now *Intruders* is a thing. Thank you! Shubnum Khan: Thank you for bringing such a delicate touch to this collection with your illustrations. I appreciate it. To the Pan Macmillan team: Thank you for believing in me and always being so awesome. I would also like to thank readers, booksellers and librarians for making my wildest dreams come true. There are so many friends who have held me together before and between *The Yearning* and *Intruders* – too many to mention – Ke leboha ho menahane. Lastly, I would like to thank my dearest Marcee for carrying my heart with her.